NIGHT OF THE

By John Russo

Based on the Screenplay by John Russo & George Romero

Copyright 1974 by John Russo
All Rights Reserved

MOVIE EMPORIUM, INC.
216 Euclid Avenue
Glassport, PA 15045

Raves for John Russo and *Night of the Living Dead*

"A double mindblower. The child in the cellar was really scary. I never experienced any kind of fear like it in my life."
—Sam Raimi

"Your book . . . guided me through my first completed movie."
—Quentin Tarantino, on *Scare Tactics*

"Full of terror, nightmares and a good time . . . very exciting . . . it scared the hell out of me."
—Tobe Hooper, director of *The Texas Chainsaw Massacre* and *Poltergeist*

"I was very taken with it. The politics of it were striking. So much going on that it wasn't a typical horror film. Even now there's power in it. It's even bolder than *Psycho*."
—John Landis, director of *An American Werewolf in London* and *Animal House*

"I screamed and cringed like everyone else. It made me realize that the horror genre could produce something really great."
—Wes Craven, director of *A Nightmare on Elm Street* and *Last House on the Left*

"I remember not being able to sleep at night. It tapped into my primal fears."
—Chris Gore, *Film Threat*

Introduction:
The Birth of the Dead

In developing the concepts and writing the screenplays and novels for *Night of the Living Dead* and *Return of the Living Dead*, our overriding concern and aim was to give true horror fans the kind of payoff they always hoped for, but seldom got, when they shelled out their hard-earned money at the ticket booth or the bookstore. This was the guiding principle that we were determined not to violate. When I say "we" I am referring to Russ Streiner, George Romero, Rudy Ricci, and others in our group who contributed to the development of the scripts and the movies.

As a teenager, I went to see just about every movie that came to my hometown of Clairton, Pennsylvania. It was a booming iron-and-coke town in those days. There were three movie theaters, and the movies changed twice a week. Often there were double features—and the price of admission was only fifty cents! I loved the *Dracula, Frankenstein,* and *Wolf Man* movies—enduring classics, sophisticated and literate explorations of supernatural horror and dread.

But I also went to see dozens of "B" horror films, always hoping, against the odds, that one of them would turn out to be surprisingly good. This almost never happened. The plots were trite, formulaic, uninspiring. Decidedly unscary.

In the fifties, because of the vaporization of Hiroshima and

Nagasaki during World War II, everyone was scared of nuclear bombs and nuclear energy—especially nuclear energy gone awry. This pervasive psychology of fear was ripe for exploitation, and it gave rise to the "mutant monster" genre of horror films. We were treated to *The Attack of the Giant Grasshopper, The Attack of the Giant Ant . . . the Giant Squid . . . the Giant Caterpillar . . .* and so on.

Did I say that the "plots" were trite? I should've said "plot" (singular) because the same plot was used over and over with each of the different mutated creatures. The giant whatever would be hinted at, but not shown in its entirety, somewhere within the first twenty or so very dull minutes. The audience at first would be teased with just a fleeting glimpse of some aspect of the monster. Then a bigger piece of it would appear to the town drunk, who was never believed by the authorities. He would usually be killed or devoured—but in such a way that nobody important ever got wise. Eventually the male and female "B" actors in the lead roles would start to catch on, but at first nobody would believe them, either. Then, during the last twenty minutes or so of the movie, our hero, who was conveniently a scientist, would figure out that the giant whatever's saliva was identical to the saliva of a commonplace caterpillar or ant or octopus or grasshopper or whatever other kind of giant mutant that had to be dealt with—and this would culminate in a "grand finale" with National Guard troops arriving in the nick of time to destroy the horrible creature with flamethrowers and grenades.

Well, we didn't want our first movie to be like that. As I said, we really wanted moviegoers to get their money's worth.

In order to do this, we had to be true to both our concept and to reality. Granted, we were working with the outlandish premise that dead people could come back to life and attack the living. But, that being the case, we realized that our characters should think and act the way real folks, ordinary folks, would think and act if they actually found themselves in that kind of situation.

As the whole world knows by now, we didn't have much money to make our first movie, and we were groping for ideas that we might be able to pull off, on an excrutiatingly limited

INTRODUCTION

budget. We made several false starts—one of these was actually a horror comedy that involved teenagers from outer space hooking up with Earth kids to play pranks and befuddle a small town full of unsuspecting adults. But we soon found out that we couldn't afford sci-fi-type special effects and we had better settle upon something that was less FX-dependent.

George Romero and I were the two writers at The Latent Image, our movie production company at that time, and we would each go to work at separate typewriters whenever we could make time; in other words, whenever we weren't making TV spots about ketchup, pickles, or beer. I said to George that whatever kind of script we came up with ought to start in a cemetery, because people were scared of cemeteries and found them spooky. I started writing a screenplay about aliens who were prowling Earth in search of human flesh. Meantime, over a Christmas break in 1967, George came up with forty pages of a story that did actually start in a cemetery and in essence was the first half of what eventually became *Night of the Living Dead*, although we didn't give it that title till after we were done shooting.

I said to George that I really liked his story. It had the right pace and feel to it, and I was hooked by the action and suspense and the twists and turns. But I was also puzzled because "You have these people being attacked, but you never say who the attackers are, so who are they?" George said he didn't know. I said, "Seems to me they could be dead people."

He said, "That's good." And then I said, "But you never say what they're after. They attack, but they don't bite, so why are they attacking?"

He said he didn't know, and I suggested, "Why don't we use my flesh-eating idea?"

So that's how the attackers in our movie became flesh-eating zombies. In our persistent striving for a good, fresh premise, we succeeded in combining some of the best elements of the vampire, werewolf, and zombie myths into one hellacious ball of wax.

Zombies weren't heavyweight fright material until we made them into flesh-eaters. In all the zombie flicks I had seen up till then—most notably Val Lewton movies like *I Walked with a Zombie*—the "walking dead" would stumble around and occasionally choke somebody or throw somebody against a wall, or maybe, in the extreme, carry off a heroine to some sort of lurid fate—but they were never as awe-inspiring as vampires or werewolves. They were meant to be scary, but they were always a little disappointing.

Night of the Living Dead struck an atavistic chord in people. It was the fear of death magnified exponentially. Not only were you afraid to die, you were afraid to become "undead." Afraid to be attacked by a dead loved one. And afraid of what you might do to your loved one if you, by being bitten, became one of the flesh-hungry undead that you feared.

Soon after our discussions, George Romero got tied up by an important commercial client and I took over screenwriting chores. That was the way we worked in those days. We spelled each other when necessary. And we all felt it was necessary to keep the ball rolling in these early stages so that our dream of making our first feature movie would not die.

In refining our concept, ideas were bandied about by me, George Romero, Russ Streiner, and others in our immediate group. Then I rewrote George's first forty pages, putting them into screenplay format, and went on to complete the second half of the script. I wanted our story to be honest, relentless, and uncompromising. I wanted to live up to the standard set by two of my favorite genre movies—the original *Invasion of the Body Snatchers* and *Forbidden Planet* (with its "monsters from the id")—and I hoped we could cause audiences to walk out of the theater with the same stunned looks on their faces that had been produced by those two classics. That is why I suggested that our indomitable hero, Ben (played by Duane Jones), should be killed by the posse that should have saved him. I said, "Pennsylvania is a big deer-hunting state, and every year three or four hundred thousand deer are shot—and ten or twelve hunters. With all these posse guys running around in the woods, gunning down ghouls, somebody is gonna be shot by accident, and wouldn't it be ironic if it's our hero?"

INTRODUCTION

This idea got incorporated into the original screenplay as did other ideas, which were implemented during filming. For instance, the "Barbra" character, played by Judith O'Dea, survives in the screenplay as written—but we decided it would be better if her brother "Johnny" came back and dragged her out of the house to be devoured.

It wasn't until 1973, after the movie had enjoyed six-plus years of phenomenal success, that I wrote the novel that was initially published by Warner Books. In the intervening years, Russ Streiner, Rudy Ricci, and I developed a screenplay for a sequel, *Return of the Living Dead*, which I later novelized. You are right now holding both original novels in your hands, appearing together for the first time, in this beautiful trade paperback.

I also wrote the novelization of Dan O'Bannon's movie version of *Return of the Living Dead*, a hit in its own right. But the totally different novel you will read now is our very first conception—of stark horror. Not a horror comedy, but stark horror in the vein of *Night of the Living Dead*.

If the dead really did arise, and if they became flesh-eaters, they might be temporarily vanquished—but like a disease that is hard to stamp out, the possibility of a renewed "plague" would always be with us. Religious cults would spring up in the wake of the undead. Maybe they would believe that the dead still needed to be burned or "spiked." And then what would happen? Would the cult's grisly expectations be realized? Would the flesh-eaters come back? This was the question that we sought to answer in a powerfully dramatic way in our follow-up story. Which is decidedly unfunny. In other words, unlike the movie, it is not a horror comedy.

If you like good, strong horror—horror that you can believe in—I welcome you to the deliciously terrifying, no-holds-barred, gloves-off world of the original *Night of the Living Dead* and *Return of the Living Dead*.

John Russo
Pittsburgh, PA
February 2010

Night of the Living Dead

Chapter 1

Think of all the people who have lived and died and will never see the trees or the grass or the sun any more.

It all seems so brief, so worth . . . nothing. Doesn't it? To live for a while and then die? It all seems to add up to so very little.

Yet in a way, it is easy to envy the dead ones.

They are beyond living, and beyond dying.

They are lucky to be dead, to be done with dying and not have to live any more. To be under the ground, oblivious . . . oblivious of hurting, oblivious of the fear of dying.

They do not have to live any more. Or die any more. Or feel pain. Or accomplish anything. Or wonder what to do next. Or wonder what it is going to be like to have to go through dying.

Why does life seem so ugly and beautiful and sad and important while you are living it, and so trivial when it is over?

Life smolders a while and then dies and the graves wait patiently to be filled, and the end of all life is death, and the new life sings happily in the breeze and neither knows nor cares anything about the old life, and then it in turn dies also.

Life is a constant turning over into graves. Things live and then die, and sometimes they live well and sometimes poorly, but they always die, and death is the one thing that reduces all things to the least common denominator.

What is it that makes people afraid of dying?
Not the pain.

Not always.
Death can be instantaneous and almost painless.
Death itself is an end to pain.
Then why are people afraid to die?
What things might we learn from those who are dead, if they find the means to return to us?
If they come back from the dead?
Will they be our friends? Or our enemies?
Will we be able to deal with them? We... who have never conquered our fear of confronting death.

At dusk, they finally spotted the tiny church. It was way back off the road, nearly hidden in a clump of maple trees, and if they had not found it before dark they probably would not have found it at all.

It was the cemetery behind the church that was the objective of their journey. And they had hunted for it for nearly two hours, down one long, winding, rural back road after another—with ruts so deep that the bottom of the car scraped and they had to crawl along at less than fifteen miles per hour, listening to a nerve-wracking staccato spray of gravel against the fenders and sweltering in a swirl of hot, yellow dust.

They had to come to place a wreath on their father's grave.

Johnny parked the car just off the road at the foot of a grassy terrace while his sister, Barbara, looked over at him and breathed a sigh intended to convey a mixture of both tiredness and relief.

Johnny said nothing. He merely tugged angrily at the knot of his already loosened tie and stared straight ahead at the windshield, which was nearly opaque with dust.

He had not turned off the engine yet, and Barbara immediately guessed why. He wanted her to suffer a while longer in the heat of the car, to impress upon her the fact that he had not wanted to make this trip in the first place and he held her responsible for all their discomfort. He was tired and disgusted and in a mood of frozen silence now, though during the two hours that they were lost he had taken his anger and resentment out on her by snapping at her continuously and refusing to be at all cheerful, while the car bounced over the ruts and he worked hard to restrain himself from ramming the gas pedal to the floor.

He was twenty-six years old and Barbara only nineteen, but she was in many ways more mature than he was—and through their growing-up years she had pretty much learned how to deal with his moods.

She merely got out of the car without a word, and left him staring at the windshield.

Suddenly the radio, which had been turned on but was not working, blurted a few words that Johnny could not understand and then was silent again. Johnny stared at the radio, then pounded on it and frantically worked the tuning knob back and forth, but he could not get another word out of it. It was strange, he thought, and just as puzzling and frustrating and tormenting as everything else that had happened to him in this totally disgusting day. It made his blood boil. If the radio was dead, then why did it blurt a few words every once in a while? It ought to be either dead or not dead, instead of being erratic or half-crazy.

He pounded the radio a few more times, and worked with the tuning knob. He thought he had heard the word "emergency" in the jumble of half-words that had come across in a squawk of static. But his pounding had no effect. The radio remained silent.

"Damn it!" Johnny said, out loud, as he yanked the keys out of the ignition and put them in his pocket and got out of the car and slammed the door.

He looked around for Barbara. Then he remembered the wreath they had brought with them to place on their father's grave, and he opened the car trunk and got it out. It was in a brown paper bag, and he tucked it under his arm as he let the trunk bang shut—and he looked for Barbara once more and experienced a burst of fresh anger at the realization that she had not bothered to wait for him.

She had scrambled up the terrace to take in a view of the church, which was tucked back into a hollow among the trees where a place had been carved for it out of the surrounding forest.

Taking his time so he wouldn't get mud on his shoes, he climbed the grassy terrace and caught up with her.

"It's a nice church," she said. "With the trees and all. It's a beautiful place."

It was a typical rural church; a wooden structure, painted white, with a red steeple and tall, narrow, old-fashioned stained-glass windows.

"Let's do what we have to do and be on our way," Johnny said, in a disgruntled tone. "It's almost dark, and we still have a three-hour drive to get home."

She shrugged at him, to show her annoyance, and he followed her around the side of the church.

There was no lawn, no gate—just tombstones, sticking up in the tall grass, under the trees, where a few scattered dead leaves crackled under their feet as they walked. The tombstones began in the grass just a few yards from the church and spread out, among trees and foliage, toward the edge of the surrounding woods.

The stones ranged in size from small identifying slates to large monuments of carefully executed design—an occasional Franciscan crucifix or a carved image of a defending angel. The oldest tombstones, grayed and browned and worn with age, almost seemed not to be tombstones at all; instead, they were like stones in the forest, blurred by the darkening silence engulfing the small rural church.

The gray sky contained a soft glow from the recent sun, so that trees and long blades of grass seemed to shimmer in the gathering night. And over it all reigned a peaceful silence, enhanced rather than disturbed by the constant rasp of crickets and the rustle of dead leaves swirling in an occasional whispering breeze.

Johnny stopped, and watched Barbara moving among the

graves. She was taking her time, being careful not to step on anybody's grave, as she hunted for the one belonging to her father. Johnny had a hunch that the idea of being in the cemetery after dark had her frightened, and the thought amused him because he was still angry with her and he wanted her to suffer just a little for making him drive two hundred miles to place a wreath on a grave—an act he considered stupid and meaningless.

"Do you remember which row it's in?" his sister called out hopefully.

But he neglected to answer her. Instead, he smiled to himself and merely watched. She continued going from stone to stone, stopping at each one that bore a hint of familiarity long enough to read the name of the deceased. She knew what her father's tombstone looked like, and she could remember also some of the names of the people buried nearby. But with the approaching darkness, she was having trouble finding her way.

"I think I'm in the wrong row," she said, finally.

"There's nobody around here," Johnny said, purposely emphasizing their aloneness. Then, he added, "If it wasn't so dark, we could find it without any trouble."

"Well, if you'd gotten up earlier . . ." Barbara said, and she let her voice trail off as she began moving down another row of graves.

"This is the last time I blow a Sunday on a gig like this," Johnny said. "We're either gonna have to move Mother out here or move the grave closer to home."

"Sometimes I think you complain just to hear yourself talk," Barbara told him. "Besides, you're just being silly. You know darned well Mother's too sick to make a drive like this all by herself."

Suddenly a familiar tombstone caught John's eye. He scrutinized it, recognized that it was their father's, and considered not telling Barbara so she would have to hunt a while longer; but his drive to get started toward home won out over his urge to torment her.

"I think that's it over there," he said, in a flat, detached tone, and he watched while Barbara crossed over to check it out, taking care not to step on any graves as she did so.

"Yes, this is it," Barbara called out. "You ought to be glad, Johnny—now we'll soon be on our way."

He came over to their father's grave and stared at the inscription briefly before taking the wreath out of the brown paper bag.

"I don't even remember what Dad looked like," he said. "Twenty-five bucks for this thing, and I don't even remember the guy very much."

"Well, I remember him," Barbara said, chastisingly, "and I was a lot younger than you were when he died."

They both looked at the wreath, which was made out of plastic and adorned with plastic flowers. At the bottom, on a piece of red plastic shaped like a ribbon tied in a large bow, the following words were inscribed in gold: "We Still Remember."

Johnny snickered.

"Mother wants to remember—so we have to drive two hundred miles to plant a wreath on a grave. As if he's staring up through the ground to check out the decorations and make sure they're satisfactory."

"Johnny, it takes you five minutes," Barbara said angrily, and she knelt at the grave and began to pray while Johnny took the wreath and, stepping close to the headstone, squatted and pushed hard to embed its wire-pronged base into the packed earth.

He stood up and brushed off his clothes, as if he had dirtied them, and continued grumbling, "It doesn't take five minutes at all. It takes three hours and five minutes. No, six hours and five minutes. Three hours up and three hours back. Plus the two hours we wasted hunting for the damned place."

She looked up from her prayer and glowered at him, and he stopped talking.

He stared down at the ground, bored. And he began to fidget, rocking nervously back and forth with his hands in his pockets. Barbara continued to pray, taking unnecessarily long it seemed to him. And his eyes began to wander, looking all around, staring into the darkness at the shapes and shadows in the cemetery. Because of the darkness, fewer of the tombstones were visible and there seemed to be not so many of them; only the larger ones could be seen clearly. And the sounds of the night seemed louder, because of the absence of human voices. Johnny stared into the darkness.

In the distance, a strange moving shadow appeared almost as a huddled figure moving among the graves.

Probably the caretaker or a late mourner, Johnny thought, and he glanced nervously at his watch. "C'mon, Barb, church was this morning," he said, in an annoyed tone. But Barbara ignored him and continued her prayer, as if she was determined to drag it out as long as possible just to aggravate him.

Johnny lit a cigarette, idly exhaled the first puff of smoke, and looked around again.

There was definitely someone in the distance, moving among the graves, Johnny squinted, but it was too dark to make out anything but an indistinct shape that more often than not blurred and merged with the shape of trees and tombstones as it advanced slowly through the graveyard.

Johnny turned to his sister and started to say something but she made the sign of the cross and stood up, ready to leave. She turned from the grave in silence, and they both started to walk slowly away, Johnny smoking and kicking at small stones as he ambled along.

"Praying is for church," he said flatly.

"Church would do you some good," Barbara told him. "You're turning into a heathen."

"Well, Grandpa told me I was damned to hell. Remember? Right here—I jumped out at you from behind that tree. Grandpa got all shook up and told me I gone be demn to yell!"

Johnny laughed.

"You used to be so scared here," he said, devilishly.

"Remember? Right here I jumped out from behind that tree at you."

"Johnny!" Barbara said, with annoyance. And she smiled to show him he was not frightening her, but she knew it was too dark for him to see the smile anyway.

"I think you're still afraid," he persisted. "I think you're afraid of the people in their graves. The dead people. What if they came out of their graves after you Barbara? What would you do? Run? Pray?"

He turned around and leered at her, as though he was about to pounce.

"Johnny, stop!"

"You're still afraid."

"No!"

"You're afraid of the dead people!"

"Stop, Johnny!"

"They're coming out of their graves, Barbara! Look! Here comes one of them now!"

He pointed toward the huddled figure which had been moving among the graves. The caretaker, or whoever it was, stopped and appeared to be looking in their direction, but it was too dark to really tell.

"He's coming to get you, Barbara! He's dead! And he's going to get you."

"Johnny, stop—he'll hear you—you're ignorant."

But Johnny ran away from her and hid behind a tree.

"Johnny, you—" she began, but in her embarrassment she cut herself short and looked down at the ground as the moving figure in the distance slowly approached her and it became obvious that their paths were going to intersect.

It seemed strange to her that someone other than she or her brother would be in the cemetery at such an odd hour.

Probably either a mourner or a caretaker.

She looked up and smiled to say hello.

And Johnny, laughing, looked out from behind his tree.

And suddenly the man grabbed Barbara around the throat and was choking her and ripping at her clothes. She tried to run or scream or fight back. But his tight fingers choked off her breath and the attack was so sudden and so vicious that she was nearly paralyzed with fear.

Johnny came running and dived at the man and tackled him—and all three fell down, Johnny pounding at the man with his fists and Barbara kicking and beating with her purse. Soon Johnny and the man were rolling and pounding at each other, while Barbara—screaming and fighting for her life—was able to wrench free.

In her panic and fear, she almost bolted.

The attacker was thrashing, pounding, seemingly clawing at all parts of Johnny's body. Johnny had all he could do to hold on. The two of them struggled to their feet, each maintaining a death grip on the other—but at the same time the attacker was like a wild animal fighting much more viciously than most men fight—beating, thrashing—even biting Johnny's hands and neck. Desperately, Johnny clutched at him and they fell in a heap.

In the total darkness, the blurred form of the two seemed to Barbara like one thrashing thing, and she feared for the outcome and she had no way of telling which one had the advantage or who was going to win or lose. She was nearly overcome with the desire to run and save herself, and yet she wanted to save her brother—but she didn't know how.

She began to scream wildly for help. And her fear became even more intense through her screaming, because part of her mind knew there was no one around and no one to hear her screams.

The two men on the ground were rolling and tumbling and slashing at each other and making animal sounds—one figure gained the advantage, and in a brief outline against the dark sky Barbara saw him slam his fists down onto the other's head.

She found a tree limb and snatched it into her hands, and took a step or two toward the fighting men.

Again, the fists came down, with a heavy dull thud and the sound of cracking bone. Barbara stopped in her tracks. The figure on top had a rock and was using it to smash his enemy's brains.

Moonlight fell across the face of the victor, and Barbara saw with a shudder of doom that it was not Johnny.

Again the heavy rock thudded into Johnny's head, as Barbara remained paralyzed with shock and fear. And then the rock fell to the earth and rolled and Barbara braced herself with her tree branch ready to use as a club, but the attacker did not rise. He continued to kneel over the vanquished body.

And Barbara heard strange ripping sounds, and she could not see clearly what the attacker was doing—but the ripping sounds continued in the night . . . ripping . . . ripping . . . as if something was being torn from Johnny's dead body.

The attacker did not seem to be concerned with Barbara . . . as her heart pounded wildly and she remained rooted with fear and the ripping sounds enveloped her and blotted out her sanity and her reason, and she was in such a state of extreme shock that she was near death and all she could hear was ripping . . . ripping . . . as the attacker wrenched and pulled at her brother's dead body and—yes!!—she saw in a fresh shaft of moonlight through a passing cloud that the attacker was sinking his teeth into Johnny's dead face.

Slowly, wide-eyed, like a woman paralyzed in a nightmare, Barbara began moving toward her brother's attacker. Her lips fell apart and involuntarily emitted a loud sob.

The attacker looked at her. And she was startled by the sound of his breath—an unearthly rasping sound. He stepped over Johnny's body and moved toward her in a half-standing position, like an animal hunched to spring.

Barbara let loose an ear-shattering scream of sheer horror, and she dropped her club and ran—the man coming after her slowly, with seeming difficulty in moving, almost as though he were crippled or maimed.

He advanced toward Barbara, making his way between the tombstones, while she ran stumbling and gasping for breath, and tumbled and rolled down the muddy, grassy terrace to the car. She yanked open the door. And she could hear the slow, muffled footsteps of her pursuer drawing nearer as she scrambled into the front seat and slammed the door shut.

No keys. The keys were in Johnny's pocket.

The attacker was moving closer, faster, more desperate to reach the girl.

Barbara clutched at the steering wheel, as though it alone might move the car. She sobbed. And almost too late she realized the windows were open—and she rolled them up frantically and locked the doors.

The attacker ripped at the door handles and pounded violently at the car.

Barbara began screaming again, but the man seemed impervious to screams and totally without fear of being caught or surprised.

He grabbed up a large stone from the road and shattered the window on the passenger side into a thousand little cracks. Another pounding blow, and the stone crashed through the window, and the man's hands were clawing at Barbara, trying to grab her by the hair, the face or the arms—anywhere.

She caught a glimpse of his face. It was death-white—and awfully contorted—as if by insanity or agonizing pain.

She smashed her fist into his face. And at the same instant she tugged at the emergency brake and pulled it loose and the car began to drift downhill, the attacker following after, pounding and ripping at the door handles and trying to hang on.

As the grade got steeper the car managed to pick up speed, and the man was shaken loose and forced to trot after it. The car went still faster and the man lost his footing and clutched at the fender, then the bumper, as he tumbled and fell heavily into the road. The car gained momentum, with Barbara's pursuer no longer hanging on. But he regained his footing and kept pursuing, resolutely, stolidly, in a slow, staggering shuffle.

The car was now plummeting down a steep, winding hill, Barbara frozen in the driver's seat, clenching the wheel, frightened by the darkness and the speed, yet too scared to slow down.

The light switch! She yanked it, and the headlights danced beams of light among the trees. She swerved to avoid crashing as the beams revealed the grade in the road and the car bounced and lurched over it and she saw that it was narrowing to one car width; and, about two hundred feet ahead, the downhill grade was going to end and an uphill grade begin.

On the uphill grade, the car slowed... and slowed... as its momentum carried it some distance up the upgrade. Barbara glanced backward, but could see nothing—then, in the dim outline of the road, the pursuing figure of her attacker rounded a bend and she knew he was moving fast after her.

On the upgrade, the car reached a full stop. Then, with a bolt of panic, Barbara realized it was starting to drift backward, carrying her toward her attacker... as he continued to draw nearer. The car picked up momentum as she sat paralyzed with fear.

Then she grabbed at the emergency brake and yanked it tight, the lurch of the car throwing her against the seat. She struggled with the door handle—but it would not budge until she remembered to pull the button up—and as the attacker drew nearer she yanked the door open and bolted from the car.

She ran.

The man behind her kept coming, desperately trying to move faster in his shuffling, staggering gait—as Barbara ran as fast as her legs could carry her up the steep grade of the gravel road. She fell. Skinned her knees. Picked herself up and kept running and the man kept coming after her.

She reached the main highway, at the top of the hill. And she kicked her shoes off and began to run faster—on hard blacktop rather than gravel—and she hoped to spot a car or truck or any kind of vehicle she could flag down. But there was nothing in sight. Then she came to a low stone wall, on the side of the road—and she knew there must be a house somewhere beyond the wall. She struggled over it and considered hiding behind it, but she could hear the rasping breath and plodding footsteps of her pursuer not too far behind her and he would be sure to look for her behind the wall—it was too obvious a hiding place.

Then, looking ahead for a moment to get her bearings, she thought she could make out a soft glow of a window in the distance, across a field and through the leafy overhanging branches of scattered trees.

In the dark, stumbling over boulders and dead branches and gnarled roots, she ran toward the lighted window across the field.

She came to a shed first, at the edge of a dirt road leading to the house. Beside the shed, illuminated in the glow of a naked light bulb swarming with gnats, stood two gasoline pumps of the type that farmers keep to supply their tractors and other vehicles. Barbara stopped and hid for a moment behind one of the pumps—until she realized that she was too vulnerable under the light from the shed.

As she turned, the light revealed her attacker coming closer, shuffling toward her across the dark field with its shrubs and trees and overhanging foliage.

She ran toward the house and began calling for help as loudly as she could yell. But no one came outside. No one came out onto the porch. The house remained silent and cold, except for the glow of light from one solitary window.

She pressed herself against the side of the house, in a darkened corner, and tried to look into the window, but she could see no signs of life, and apparently no one had heard her screams and no one was coming out to help her.

Silhouetted in the glow of light from the shed, the man who killed her brother was drawing nearer.

In panic, she ran to the rear of the house and into the shadows of a small back porch. Her first impulse was to cry again for help, but she silenced herself in favor of trying to stay hidden. She gasped, realized how loud her breathing was, and tried to hold her breath. Silence. Night sounds . . . and the sound of the wild beating of her heart . . . did not stop her from hearing her attacker's running footsteps slowing to a trot... then a slow walk. And finally the footsteps stopped.

Barbara glanced quickly about. She spied a rear window and peered through it, but inside everything was dark. The pursuing footsteps resumed again, louder and more ominous. She pressed herself back against the door of the house, and her hand fell on the doorknob. She looked down at it, sure that it was locked, but grabbed it with a turn, and the door opened.

Chapter 2

She entered quickly, as quietly as possible, and closed the door softly behind her, bolting it and feeling in the darkness for a key. Her hand found a skeleton key and she turned it, making a barely audible rasp and click. She leaned against the door, listening, and could still hear the distant footfalls of the man approaching and trying to seek her out.

A tremble shot through her as she groped in the darkness and her hand touched the cold burner of an electric stove. The kitchen. She was in the kitchen of the old house. She pressed a button and the stove light came on, giving her enough illumination to scrutinize her surroundings without, she hoped, alerting her pursuer to where she was. For several seconds, she maintained a controlled silence and did not move a muscle. Then she got the nerve to move.

She crossed the kitchen into a large living room, unlighted and devoid of any signs of life. Her impulse was to call for help again, but she stopped herself for fear of being heard by the man outside. She darted back to the kitchen, rummaged through drawers in a kitchen cabinet, and found the silverware. She chose a large steak knife and, grasping it tightly, went to listen at the door again. All was quiet. She crept back into the living room. Beyond it she could dimly make out an alcove that contained the front entrance to the house. Seized with panic, she bolted to the front door and made sure it was locked. Then, cautiously, she peeled back a corner of the curtain to see outside. The view revealed the expansive lawn and grassy field she had run across earlier, with its large shadowy trees and shrubs and the shed and gasoline pumps lit up in the distance. Barbara could neither see nor hear any sign of her attacker.

Suddenly there was a noise from outside: the pounding and rattling of a door. Barbara dropped the curtain edge and stiffened. More sounds. She hurried to a side window. Across the lawn, she saw that the man was pounding at the door to the garage. She watched, her eyes wide with fear. The man continued to pound savagely at the door, then looked about and picked up something and smashed at it. In panic, Barbara pulled away from the window and flattened herself against the wall.

Her eyes fell on a telephone, across the room on a wooden shelf. She rushed to it and picked up the receiver. Dial tone. Thank God. She frantically dialed the operator. But the dial tone stopped and there was dead silence. Barbara depressed the buttons of the phone again and again, but she could not get the dial tone to resume. Just dead silence. For some reason, the phone was out of order. The radio. The phone. Out of order.

She slammed the receiver down and rushed to another window. A figure was crossing the lawn, coming toward the house. It seemed to be a different figure, a different man. Her heart leapt with both fear and hope—because she did not know who the new man could be, and she dared not cry out to him for help.

She ran to the door and peered out through the curtains again, anxious for a clue as to whether this new person in the yard might be friend or foe. Whoever he was, he was still walking toward the house. A shadow fell suddenly across a strip of window to the left of the door, and Barbara started and jumped back because of its abruptness.

She peeled back a corner of the window curtain and saw the back of the first attacker not ten feet away, facing the other man who was fast approaching. The attacker moved toward the new man, and Barbara did not know what to expect next. She froze against the door and glanced down at her knife—then looked back out at the two men.

They joined each other, seemingly without exchange of words, under the dark, hanging trees, and stood quietly, looking back toward the cemetery. From inside the house, Barbara squinted, trying to see. Finally, the attacker moved back across the road, in the direction of the cemetery. The other man approached the house and stopped in the shadow of a tree, stolidly watching.

Barbara peered into the darkness, but could see little. She lunged toward the phone again, picked up the receiver, and heard dead silence. She barely stopped herself from slamming down the receiver.

Then suddenly came a distant sound—an approaching car. She scampered to the window and looked out, holding her breath. The road seemed empty. But after a moment a faint light appeared, bouncing and rapidly approaching—a car coming up the road. Barbara reached for the doorknob and edged the door open ever so slightly, allowing a little light to spill out over the lawn. There, under a large old tree, was the unmistakable silhouette of the second man. Barbara shuddered, choked with fear at the thought of making a break for the approaching car. The man under the tree appeared to be sitting quite still, his head and shoulders slumped over, though his gaze seemed to be directed right at the house.

Barbara allowed the car to speed by, while she just stared at the hated figure in the lawn. Her chance to run was gone. She closed the door and backed into the shadows of the house. It dawned on her that perhaps the first attacker had gone for reinforcements, and they would return en masse to batter the door down and rape her and kill her.

She glanced frantically all around her. The large, dreary room was very quiet, cast in shadow. Between the living room and the kitchen, there was a hallway and a staircase; she moved toward it stealthily and her fingers found a light switch. The light at the top of the stairs came on, and she ascended the staircase, clinging to the banister for support and hoping desperately to be able to find a place to hide. She tiptoed... tiptoed... keeping a firm grip on the handle of her knife, and then, as she reached the top of the landing, she screamed—an ear-shattering scream that ripped through her lungs and echoed through the old house—because, there, on the floor at the top of the landing, under the glow of the naked light bulb in the hall, was a corpse with the flesh ripped from its bones and its eyes missing from their sockets and the white teeth and cheekbones bared and no longer covered by skin, as if the corpse had been eaten by rats, as it lay there in its pool of dried blood.

Screaming in absolute horror, Barbara dropped her knife and ran and tumbled down the stairs. In full flight now, gagging and almost vomiting, with her brain leaping at the edge of sheer madness, she wanted to get out of that house—and she broke for the door and unlocked it and flung herself out into the night, completely unmindful of the consequences.

Suddenly she was bathed in light that almost blinded her—and as she threw her arms up to protect herself, there was a loud screeching sound, and as she struggled to run, a man jumped in front of her.

"Are you one of them?" the man shouted.

She stared, frozen.

The man standing in front of her had leaped out of a pick-up truck that he had driven onto the lawn and stopped with a screech of brakes and a jounce of glaring headlights.

Barbara stared at him, but no words would come to her lips.

"Are you one of them?" he yelled again. "I seen 'em to look like you!"

Barbara shuddered. He had his arm raised, about to strike her, and she could not make out his features because he was silhouetted against the bright headlights of the truck.

Behind the truck driver, the man under the tree took a few steps forward. Barbara screamed and stepped back, and the truck driver turned to face the advancing man—who stopped and watched and did not resume his advance.

Finally the truck driver grabbed Barbara and shoved her back into the living room so forcefully that she fell down with his body on top of her, and she closed her eyes and prepared to accept her death.

But he got off of her and slammed the door shut and locked it. And he lifted the curtains and peered out. He did not seem to be very much concerned about her, so she finally opened her eyes and stared at him.

He was carrying a tire iron in his hand. He was a black man, perhaps thirty years old, dressed in slacks and a sweater. He did not at all resemble her attacker. In fact, though his face bore an intense look, it was friendly and handsome. He appeared to be a strong man, well over six feet tall.

Barbara got to her feet and continued to stare at him.

"It's all right," he said, soothingly. "It's all right. I ain't one of those creeps. My name is Ben. I ain't going to hurt you."

She sank into a chair and began to cry softly, while he concerned himself with his surroundings. He moved into the next room and checked the locks on the windows. He turned on a lamp; it worked; and he turned it back off.

He called to Barbara from the kitchen.

"Don't you be afraid of that creep outside! I can handle him all right. There's probably gonna be lots more of them, though, soon as they find out we're here. I'm out of gas, and the gasoline pumps out back are locked. Do you have the key?"

Barbara did not reply.

"Do you have the key?" Ben repeated, trying to control his anger.

Again, Barbara said nothing. Her experiences of the past couple of hours had brought her to a state of near-catatonia.

Ben thought maybe she did not hear, so he came into the living room and addressed her directly.

"I said the gas pumps out back are locked. Is there food around here? I'll get us some food, then we can beat off that creep out there and try to make it somewhere where there is gas."

Barbara merely held her face in her hands and continued to cry.

"I guess you tried the phone," Ben said, no longer expecting an answer. And he picked it up and fiddled with it but could not get anything but dead silence, so he slammed it down into its cradle. He looked at Barbara and saw she was shivering.

"Phone's no good," he said. "We might as well have two tin cans and a string. You live here?"

She remained silent, her gaze directed toward the top of the stairs. Ben followed her stare and started toward the stairs, but halfway up he saw the corpse—and stared for a moment and slowly backed down into the living room.

His eyes fell on Barbara, and he knew she was shivering with shock, but there was nothing for him to do but force himself back into action.

"We've got to bust out of here," he said. "We've got to find some other people—somebody with guns or something."

He went into the kitchen and started rummaging, flinging open the refrigerator and the cupboards. He began filling a shopping bag with things from the refrigerator, and because he was in a hurry he literally hurled the things into the bag.

Suddenly, to his surprise, he looked up and Barbara was standing beside him.

"What's happening?" she said, in a weak whisper, so weak that Ben almost did not hear. And she stood there wide-eyed, like a child waiting for an answer.

Amazed, he stared at her.

"What's happening?" she repeated, weakly, shaking her head in fright and bewilderment.

Suddenly they were both startled by a shattering crash. Ben dropped the groceries, seized his jack-handle, and ran to the front door and looked out through the curtained window. Another shattering sound. The first attacker had joined the second man at the old pick-up truck, and with rocks the two had smashed out the headlights.

"Two of them," Ben muttered to himself, and as he watched, the two men outside started to beat with their rocks at the body of the truck—but their beating seemed to have no purpose; it seemed to be just mindless destruction. In fact, outside of smashing the headlights, they were not harming the old truck very much.

But Ben spun around with a worried look on his face.

"They're liable to wreak the engine," he said to Barbara. "How many of them are out there? Do you know?"

She backed away from him, and he lunged at her and grabbed her by the wrists and shook her, in an effort to make her understand.

"How many? Come on, now—I know you're scared. But I can handle the two that are out there now. Now, how many are there? That truck is our only chance to get out of here. How many? How many?"

"I don't know! I don't know!" she screamed. "What's happening? I don't know what's happening!"

As she struggled to break his hold on her wrists, she burst into hysterical sobbing.

Ben turned away from her and moved for the door. He lifted the curtain and looked out for a moment. The attackers were still beating at the truck, wildly trying to tear it apart.

Ben flung open the door, and leaped off of the porch, and began cautiously advancing toward the two men. As they turned to face him, he was revolted by what he saw in the glow of the light from the living room of the old house.

The faces of the attackers were the faces of humans who were dead. The flesh on their faces was rotting and oozing in places. Their eyes bulged from deep sockets. Their flesh was bloodless and pasty white. They moved with an effort, as though whatever force had brought them to life had not done a complete job. But they were horrible, ghoulish beings, and they frightened Ben to the depths of his ability to be frightened, as he moved toward them brandishing his jack-handle.

"Come and get it, now. Come and get it," Ben muttered to himself, as he concentrated on his attack, moving forward stolidly at first, then breaking almost into a run.

But the two, instead of backing off, moved toward the man, as though drawn by some deep-seated urge. Ben pounded into them, swinging his jack-handle again and again with all his might. But his blows, powerful though they were, seemed to have little effect. He couldn't stop the things, or hurt them. It was like beating a rug; every time he flung them back they advanced again, in a violent, brutal struggle. But Ben finally managed to beat them to the ground, and for a long while he continued to pound at their heads, at their limp forms lying there on the lawn, until he was almost sobbing with each of his blows, beating and beating at them, while Barbara stood on the porch and watched in a state of shock. Over and over, he drove the jack-handle smashing into the skulls of the prostrate creatures—humanoids, or whatever they were—until the sheer violence of it set Barbara off on a rampage of screaming—screaming and holding her head and trying to cover her eyes. Again and again her screams pierced the night, mingled with Ben's sobs and the sounds of the jack-handle hammering into the skulls of the dead things.

Ben finally got hold of himself, and stopped. Breathing heavily, he stood, enveloped in the quiet of the night.

Silent now, the girl stood in the doorway and looked at him—or through him—he could not be sure which. He turned to face her and say something to comfort her, but he could not get his breath.

Suddenly, he heard a noise behind the girl, from inside the house. He leaped up onto the porch, and walking toward her from the kitchen was another of the horrible dead things. Somehow it must have broken the bolt on the kitchen door.

"Lock that door!" Ben yelled and Barbara summoned the presence of mind to shut the living-room door and lock it, as still another brutal struggle ensued in the living room.

The dead thing that Ben began struggling with this time was

more horrible-looking than the other two, as if it had been dead longer, or had died a more terrible death. Patches of hair and flesh had been torn from its head and face, and the bones of its arms showed through the skin like a jacket with the elbows worn through. And one dead eye was hanging halfway out of its socket, and its mouth was twisted and caked with blood and dirt.

Ben tried to hit it, but the thing grabbed onto Ben's arm, and the jack-handle dropped to the floor. Ben groped and struggled with the thing, and finally twisted it around and wrestled it down onto the carpet. The thing was emitting strange rasping sounds from its dead throat, like the sounds that had been made by whoever had killed Barbara's brother . . . and it raked its hands in the direction of Ben's throat—but it did not make contact, because Ben had seized the jack-handle and he drove it point first into the thing's skull.

Ben stood up. He had to use his foot against the dead thing's head to gain leverage to pull the jack-handle out—and the dead skull flopped back with a thud against the living-room floor. And just the tiniest bit of fluid, white and not the color of blood, oozed from the wound made by the jack-handle in the dead creature's skull.

But Ben had no time to think of what it might mean, because a sound in the kitchen told him that still another of the things had gotten in. He met it in the hall and with powerful jack-handle blows drove it out beyond the kitchen door so that he could fall against it, shutting it and leaning against it to keep it shut while he tried to get his breath.

After a long silence, Ben said, "They know we're in here now. It's no secret any longer, if it ever was. And they're going to kill us if we don't protect ourselves."

He spoke directly to Barbara, as though looking for a sign that she understood and would cooperate in their struggle to survive. But she did not hear him. Her face was twitching in fright, and her eyes remained wide open in a non-blinking stare.

She was staring toward the floor, at the spot where the dead humanoid lay. It was askew on its back, in the hallway between the living room and the kitchen, its right arm jutting at a crazy angle toward the girl with fingers twisted as though to grab.

Horrified, Barbara thought she saw a slight movement in the thing's hand. It twitched. The whole body twitched slightly—the bent, broken neck keeping the being's head twisted upward, in an open-mouthed, one-eyed glassy stare.

As if in a trance, Barbara took a few steps toward the thing, the fear in her face contorting into a sick frown. And the hand twitched again. The girl moved toward it, drawn toward it, staring down at it with overpowering curiosity.

The dead thing lay there twitching and staring, with the one eye hanging out and the beginnings of decay on its face and neck.

But Barbara moved closer, and the thing continued to twitch, its one eye still staring upward, glassy and pale, like the eye of a stuffed animal.

Adrenaline coursed through Barbara's body, as she felt an overpowering drive to run or scream, even though she remained rooted, fixatedly staring into the eye of the dead thing. And suddenly it moved, with a rustling sound. And Barbara jumped and screamed, jolted out of her trance, before the realization came to her that Ben had a hold on the thing's legs and was dragging it across the floor.

"Shut your eyes, girl, I'm getting this dead thing out of here," Ben said, in a stern voice, and his face showed his anguish and revulsion as he dragged the dead body across the floor.

The one eye continued to twitch. And Barbara just stood there, her hands still at her mouth, watching, listening to the sounds of Ben's breathing and his struggling with the dead being. Finally, he got the body to the kitchen door, and he let the legs drop with a thud as he paused to rest and think.

Even in the dim illumination provided by the stove light, Barbara could see the shiny perspiration on Ben's face, and the rasp of his heavy breathing seemed to fill the room. His eyes were alert, and afraid. He turned quickly to see through the small window pane in the door. The dead thing still lay twitching slightly at his feet.

And outside, lurking in the shadow from the huge trees, Ben's probing eyes discerned three more beings watching and waiting, their arms dangling and eyes bulging, as they maintained a dumb, fixated stare in the direction of the house.

With a swift move, the big man flung open the kitchen door and bent to pick up the dead thing at his feet. The three ghoulish creatures outside under the trees began to take slow, shuffling, threatening steps toward the house. And, with one great heave, Ben flopped the dead, twitching form outside the door, just beyond the threshold.

The things on the lawn continued to advance, as the rasp of crickets mingled with the agonized, bellows-like rasping of their dead lungs, nearly obliterating all the other night sounds.

With another great effort, Ben heaved the dead but twitching body over the edge of the porch.

From inside the house, the big man's efforts could not be clearly discerned by Barbara, and she backed away from the door and trembled uncontrollably while she waited for Ben to finish whatever he was going to do and come back inside.

He shuddered and fumbled in his breast pocket, as the ghoulish beings on the lawn continued to move toward him with their arms extended, reaching out as though to seize him and tear him apart. Ben's fumbling fingers closed on a book of matches, and he managed to strike one and touch the burning tip to the ragged, filthy clothing of the dead thing, and with almost a popping sound the clothing caught fire.

The things in the yard stopped in their tracks. The fire blazed slowly at first. Shaking, Ben touched the match to other aspects of the thing's clothing and, intent on the advancing ghouls, he burned his fingers and snapped them, tossing the match into the heaped form. Standing, and breathing hard, he kicked the burning thing off the edge of the porch and watched it roll down three small steps onto the grass, where it lay still, the flames licking around it.

Ben watched the three beings in the yard as they stepped back slightly, trying to cover their faces with their stiff arms, as though they were afraid of fire—and his fists clenched the banister of the little porch as his face glowed in the heat of the flames.

"I'm going to get you," Ben said to himself, his voice quivering. And then he raised his voice and shouted into the deadness of the night, "I'm going to get you! All of you! You damned things!"

Ben stood defiantly on the little porch, the flaming corpse burning with an overpowering stench. Yet, the things on the lawn had stopped backing away, and they were keeping their distance now—watching and waiting.

Hearing a sudden noise, Ben spun to see Barbara standing inside the kitchen door. As his eyes met hers, he took in the blank, frozen expression on her face, and she backed away from him into the room. The big man, in great strides, re-entered the kitchen and slammed the door and reflexively went to bolt it, but the bolt had been broken loose by the things that had gotten in.

Ben seized hold of a heavy kitchen table, and dragged it and slammed it against the door. His breathing still loud, was even more rapid than before. And his eyes continually darted about the room in search of something—but Barbara did not know what.

He rushed to the cabinets and threw them open and began rummaging through them. They were full of standard kitchen utensils and supplies. For a long time, Ben did not speak—and Barbara's staring eyes followed him about as he continued to ransack the room.

"See if you can find the light switch," he shouted suddenly—so suddenly that the sound of his voice startled Barbara and she fell back against a wall and her hand groped to a switch. The light from an overhead fixture came on, providing bright illumination. The big man continued to clatter about frantically, while the light coming on hurt Barbara's eyes and caused her to blink and squint. She remained against the wall, her hand still touching the switch, as though she did not dare to move. She watched silently, while Ben continued flinging open drawers and spilling contents onto the shelving and onto the floor.

He grabbed the silverware drawer, still open from when Barbara first discovered it, and pulled it open until it stopped itself with a crash. He rooted through it, pulled out a large bread knife and, sucking his breath in, stuffed it under his belt. Then he reached into the drawer again and produced another knife. Taking Barbara by surprise, he strode toward her and shoved the knife at her, handle first, but she backed away from him—and her action stayed his franticness and, breathing heavily through his words, he calmed himself and spoke softly but commandingly to her.

"Now . . . you hang on . . . to this."

She hesitated, but finally took the knife, and he breathed a sigh of relief. She seemed weak, almost apathetic, as though she was losing control of herself—or had given up already. She stared at the weapon in her hand, then her eyes came up to meet the man's intense face.

"All right," he said. "All right. You just listen to me, and we're gonna be okay. We have to protect ourselves—keep those things away from us, until we can find a way to get out of this damned place."

He did not know if his words penetrated through to Barbara or not, but hopefully they did.

He pulled away from her and continued to rummage, speaking only occasionally and to no one in particular between great breaths and between the brief times when his interest was totally wrapped in something found in his rummaging—something useful or potentially useful for survival.

His search was not without control; it had a coordinated purpose; it was selective, although frantic and desperate. He was looking for nails and strips of wood or planks that he might nail around doors and windows. He had made up his mind that they were going to have to fortify the old farmhouse as strongly as possible, against the impending and gathering threat of an all-out attack by the ghouls, which were increasing in number. Ben's actions were hurried, and intent after these defensive ends; at first, his search occupied his full attention and was driven by anxiety. But gradually, as he moved about and began to come up with several key items, his efforts paced down into a more deliberate flow.

He started bracing heavy tables and other articles of furniture against the most vulnerable parts of the old house.

His mood relaxed in intensity and became calmer, more analytical, as the barricading instilled a feeling of greater security. And the knowledge of the efforts toward some safety and some protection began to overtake Barbara, bringing her out of her shock and passivity.

"We'll be okay!" Ben called out, in an effort at bravery.

And Barbara watched, as he clattered about the room, spilling his findings out of drawers and off of shelves. He still had not apparently found at least one important item that he was really impatient for. Spools of thread, buttons, manicure implements, shoe-shine materials... continued to spill out of drawers. And Ben got once more a little violent and urgent as he continued to rummage and bang around the room.

Finally, in a wooden box under the sink, he found what he was looking for—and he leaped suddenly and let out an exclamation of triumph as he dumped the contents of the box onto the kitchen floor. A big claw hammer thudded out. And an axe. And an old pipe tobacco tin, which Ben seized and in one gesture spilled its contents onto a shelf. Nails and screws and washers and tacks tumbled out. A few rolled too far and clattered onto the floor, but Ben dived and his fingers scooped them up. He fumbled through the little pile of things and selected the longest nails in the batch, and stuffed them into the pocket of his sweater. And even as he stuffed the nails into his pocket, he was already moving, his eyes seeking for his next need.

His eyes fell on Barbara.

"See if there's any big pieces of wood around the fireplace out there!" he yelled at her, and he turned to explore the contents of a cardboard box on top of the refrigerator. The box came up too easily, telling him it was empty, and he flung it down with a glance inside to make sure, as his impetus carried him toward a metal cabinet in the corner of the room which he was betting would contain nothing but foodstuffs—but in turning he noticed Barbara, still motionless, and his anger leaped to the surface suddenly and he shouted at her.

"Look, you—"

But he stopped himself, then spoke still frantically, but with less harshness.

"Look... I know you're scared. I'm scared, too. I'm scared just like you. But we're not gonna survive... if we don't do something to help ourselves. I'm going to board up these doors and windows. But you've got to pitch in. We've got to help ourselves, because there ain't nobody around to help us... and we're gonna be all right. Okay? Now, I want you to get out there and see if there's any wood in that fireplace..."

He stopped, still breathing hard. Barbara merely stared at him. Then, after several seconds, she started to move, very slowly, away from the wall.

"Okay?" Ben asked, looking into her eyes.

She was still for a long moment, before nodding her head weakly.

"Okay," Ben repeated, reassuringly, in a half-whisper, and he stared after the girl momentarily as she left the kitchen—and he continued his search.

She moved into the living-room area, where the darkness stopped her for an instant, slowing her pace. From the kitchen, she could still hear the clattering sounds of Ben's search. She looked ahead, into the room, and clutched the handle of her knife as the white curtains on the windows seemed to glow, and every shadow seemed suspect. Anything could be lurking in that room, behind the furniture, or in the closets.

Barbara shuddered.

On the dining table in the far corner of the room, she could see the silhouette of a bowl of large rounded flowers—and they stirred suddenly, in the breeze from an opened window. In a panic, Barbara raced for the window and slammed it shut and bolted it, and stood, breathing heavily and noticing that she had pinned part of the white curtain under the window frame when it came crashing down. But she was not going to raise it back up again, for anything. A shiver shot through her, and she turned to see Ben, who had come as far as the doorway to find out the cause of the noise—and she hoped he would stay, but he turned and resumed his banging around in the kitchen.

Alone in the room again, Barbara reached for a lamp on an end table, clicked it on and dull illumination filled the immediate area. The room felt empty. She started slowly toward the fireplace. Near it was a stack of logwood, and a few planks that might be large enough to nail across the windows. Still clutching her knife, she bent over the pile and gathered up the planking—but a spider ran across her hand, and she shrieked and dropped the wood with a clatter.

She waited, hoping Ben would not come, and this time he did not come to see what was the matter. Loud continuous noises of his activity in the kitchen told her why he had not heard her own racket with the firewood. She knelt and picked the planks up again, and steeled her mind not to be frightened by spiders.

Staggering with her awkward load, she hurried toward the kitchen and, bursting through the doorway, she found Ben pounding with the claw hammer at the hinges on a tall broom-closet door. One final swipe and a great yank freed the door, with the sound of screws ripping from torn wood, and the man stood it against the wall next to the broom closet. In the recesses of the closet, he spotted other useful items and pulled them out—an ironing board, three center boards from the dining table, and some old scrap lumber.

He smiled at Barbara when he looked up and saw her own supply of wood, which she leaned against the wall in a corner, and motioning for her to follow he grabbed the closet door and carried it across the kitchen to the back door of the house, which was the door with the broken bolt. He slapped the closet door up against the panel portion of the kitchen door and with an appraising glance he realized that he could use this same piece to cover the kitchen window, which was of modest dimensions and not placed too far from the kitchen door. He leaned against the piece of wood and groped in his sweater pocket for nails. The door started to slip slightly. It was not going to completely cover the kitchen window, but it would leave slats of glass at top and bottom; however, it would cover the glass part of the entrance door and would help make the door secure. Again, the heavy closet door slipped and he nudged it back into position, as he continued to grope for nails. Suddenly springing forward, Barbara helped out, by taking hold of the piece of lumber and holding it in position. Ben accepted her help automatically, without recognition, and gave the barricade a cursory inspection as he determined where to sink the nails; then, pulling several long nails from his pocket, he placed them and drove them in with swift, powerful blows from the claw hammer. He drove two on his side through the door and molding, then moved swiftly to her side and drove two more. Then, with the weight of the piece supported, he pounded the nails until they were completely sunken and stood back and began to add more. He wanted to use the nails sparingly but wisely, where they would do the most good, because he did not have an unlimited supply.

He tugged at the kitchen door, and it now seemed secure enough, and with the first defensive measures undertaken and accomplished, Ben began to take on confidence and assurance. He was still scared, and he continued to work quickly and, he hoped, wisely—and the fact that he had tools to work with and a plan to put into effect to maintain survival gave him the feeling that he was not entirely helpless and there were strong, positive things he could do to bring his and the girl's destiny under control.

"There! By God!" he said, finally, in a burst of self confidence. "That ought to hold those damn things and stop them from getting in here. They ain't that strong—there!"

And he drove two more nails into the molding around the kitchen window. And when he tugged at the barricade, it again seemed plenty secure.

"They ain't coming through that," Ben said, and he gave the nails a few final blows, until the heads sunk into the wood.

His eyes scrutinized the parts of the glass that remained uncovered, but they were not sufficiently wide for a human body to pass through. "I don't have too many nails," Ben said. "I'll leave that for now. It's more important to fix up some of the other places where they can get in."

Barbara did not respond to any of his talking, neither to add encouragement nor advice, and he turned from the barricade with an exasperated glance in her direction before standing back and once more surveying the room. There were no other doors or windows except the door leading to the living room.

"Well . . . this place is fairly secure," Ben said, tentatively, and he looked to Barbara for some sign of approval, but she remained silent, so Ben continued, raising the volume of his voice in an attempt to hammer home the meaning of what he was saying. "Now . . . if we have to . . ."

The girl just stood and watched him.

"If we have to . . . we just run in here—and no dragging now, or I'm gonna leave you out there to fend for yourself. If they get into any other part of the house, we run in here and board up this door."

He meant the door between the kitchen and the living room, which had been open all along. Barbara watched while he closed it, tested it, then shut it tight.

He opened it again, then quickly chose several of the lumber strips and stood them against the wall where he intended to leave them in case it became an emergency to board up the living-room door.

He groped in his pocket and realized his supply of nails was dwindling and he moved to the shelf to check the pile of stuff he had spilled from the tobacco can; he emptied the can completely and dug into the contents for all of the longest nails and tossed just those ones back into the can. Then he handed the can to Barbara.

"You take these," he said, and his voice left no room for argument or hesitation.

She reacted quickly, as though she had been jolted out of a reverie, and took the tobacco tin from Ben's big hand. She watched as he gathered as much of the lumber as he could carry into his arms and started out of the room. She did not want to be left alone, and he had not told her to remain in the kitchen, so she followed silently after him, carrying the tobacco tin in front of her as though she was not sure why she was doing it.

They entered the living room.

"It ain't gonna be too long," Ben said, breathing heavily. "They're gonna be trying to pound their way in here. They're afraid now . . . I think . . . or maybe they just ain't hungry . . ."

He dropped his load of wood in the middle of the floor and walked over to the large front windows, talking as he moved. His tone of voice was suddenly intense, and his speech rapid.

"They're scared of fire, too—I found that out."

Still standing dumbly in the center of the room holding her knife in one hand and the tobacco tin in the other, Barbara watched as Ben stepped forward and his eye measured the size of the big windows. He looked all around the room—and finally his eyes fixed on the large dining table and he moved quickly toward it, talking as he moved, resuming his train of thought.

"There must've been fifty, maybe a hundred of those things down in Cambria when the news broke."

Barbara watched, almost transfixed. At his mention of the number of the things, her eyes reflected amazement and frightened curiosity. Ben dragged the heavy table away from the wall, then walked around it studying its size, and hoisted one end and turned it onto its side. Bracing it against himself, he heaved on one of the legs and tried to break it free. With a great ripping sound, the table leg came loose, after a tremendous effort on Ben's part, and he dropped it onto the rug—with a loud, heavy thud. He continued talking, breathing heavily and perspiring as he worked, punctuating his remarks with vengeance on the table as he ripped all the legs off, one by one.

"I saw a big gasoline truck, you know... down at Beekman's? Beekman's diner. And I heard the radio—there's a radio in the truck..."

He wrenched at the second table leg. It cracked loudly but did not come free. He moved to where the claw hammer lay, in the middle of the floor.

"This gasoline truck came screaming out of the diner lot onto the road—must've been ten... fifteen... of those things chasing it—but I didn't see them right away—they were on the other side of the truck. And it looked strange, the way the truck was moving so fast... instead of taking its time pulling out of the diner and onto the road."

POW! POW!

With two powerful swats of the claw hammer, he freed the second table leg, and it clattered to the floor. Ben tossed it into the corner, and moved to the third leg.

"I just saw this big truck at first—and it looks funny how fast it's coming out onto the road. And then I saw those things—and the truck was moving slower, and they were catching up... and grabbing... and jumping on. They had their arms around the driver's neck..."

Another table leg fell loose and thudded to the rug. Ben was breathing very hard. And Barbara was listening, both horrified and fascinated by his story.

"And that truck just cut right across the road—through the guard rail, you know. And I had to hit my brakes, and I went screeching all over the place, and the truck smashed into a big sign and into the pumps of the Sunoco station down there. I heard the crash. And that big thing started burning—and yet it was still moving, right through the pumps and on into the station—and I'm stopped, dead in my tracks. And I saw those things... and they all started to back off... some of them running... or trying to run... but they run kind of like they're crippled. But they keep backing off. And it's like... it's like they gotta get away from the fire—and the guy driving the truck couldn't get out nohow—the cab of the truck was plowed halfway into the wall of the Sunoco station—and he's being burned alive in there and he's screaming—screaming like hell..."

Barbara's eyes deepened, and her face wrinkled in anxiety. The continuing nightmare, for her, was growing more and more complex.

Ben swatted the last table leg from the table, and the table top started to drop. It was heavy. He regained control of it and struggled, trying to drag it across the room. Barbara moved toward him and took hold of an end of the table, but did not really help much, as it was really too heavy for her to pitch in.

"I don't know what's gonna happen," Ben said. "I mean, I didn't know if the gas station was going to explode... or fly to pieces... or what's gonna happen. I just started driving down the road, trying to get far away in case there was an explosion... and the guy in the truck is screaming and screaming... and after a while he just stops."

He set down the table, and wiped beads of perspiration from his forehead. His breathing was still heavy from the previous exertion. He wiped his hand on his shirt. His eyes were wide and angry with the remembrance of the events he was describing for Barbara, and it almost seemed as though he might weep.

"And there those things were... standing back... across the road... standing looking like... looking like... like they just came back from the grave or something. And they were over by the diner, and there was cars and buses in the diner lot, with lots of windows smashed. And I knew those things must've finished off all the people in the diner, and more were outside, all over the place just biding their time for a chance to move in. So I went barreling right across the road in my truck—and I drove it right at some of those things—and I got a good look at them, I saw them for the first time in my lights—and then... I just run right down on them—and I grind down as hard as I can—and I knock a couple of them about fifty feet, flailin' into the air. And I just wanted to crush them—smash them filthy things. And they're just standing there. They don't bother to run. They don't even bother to get out of the road. Some of them keep reaching out, as if they could grab me. But they're just standing there... and the truck is running them down... as if... as if they were a bunch of bugs..."

Seeing the fear in Barbara's eyes, Ben stopped himself. She was wide-eyed, staring in disgust, her hands still resting on the table top.

He refocused his attention on the table top, and started to lift it again. Barbara was practically motionless. As he tugged on the table, her hands fell away and she slowly pulled them against herself. He dragged the table, unassisted, toward the window he intended to board up with it.

He looked at Barbara. She stared back, practically expressionless.

"I'm just... I... I got kids," Ben said rubbing his perspiring forehead with his sleeve. "And... I guess they'll do all right. They can take care of themselves... but they're still only kids... and I'm being away and all... and..."

His voice trailed off, as he had gotten no response from Barbara and didn't know what to say next. He tugged at the table, and allowed it to lean against the wall.

"I'm just gonna do what I can," he said, making an effort to sound positive. "I'm going to do what I can, and I'm gonna get back... and I'm gonna see my people. And things are gonna be all right... and... I'm gonna get back."

His talk had begun to repeat itself, and he realized he had started to babble, and he saw the girl intently watching him, and he stopped. He composed himself with some effort, and started to speak a little more slowly. His voice became almost a monotone, with enforced calm, but beneath his anger and his fear he was a brave man, and he was bound and determined not to lose his confidence. He knew the girl was in need of bolstering, if she was going to be able to cope with the situation. Like it or not, his survival was to some measure dependent on hers, and on how well he could get her to cooperate and overcome her fear.

"Now, you and me are gonna be all right, too," he told her. "We can hold those things off. I mean . . . you can just . . . smash them. All you have to do is just keep your head and don't be too afraid. We can move faster than they can, and they're awfully weak compared to a grown man . . . and if you don't run and just keep swinging at them . . . you can smash them. We're smarter than they are. And we're stronger than they are. We're gonna stop them. Okay?"

The girl stared.

"All we have to do is just keep our heads," Ben added.

They looked at each other for a moment, until Ben turned and picked up the table top again. As he started hoisting it up to the window, the girl spoke, quietly and weakly.

"Who are they?"

Ben stopped in his tracks, still supporting the heavy table top, and looked with amazement at Barbara's anxious face. Slowly, it dawned on him that the girl had never been really aware of the thing that had been happening. She had no idea of the extent of the danger, or the reason for it. She had not heard the radio announcements, the bulletins. She had been existing in a state of uninformed shock.

Incredulously, Ben shouted, "You haven't heard anything?"

She stared blankly, silently, her eyes fastened on his. Her reply was in her silence.

"You mean you don't have any idea what's going on?"

Barbara started to nod her answer, but instead she was seized with a fit of trembling. "I . . . I . . ."

Her trembling increased, she began to shake violently, and suddenly she flung her arms up and flailed them about, sobbing wildly. She began to walk in panic, wildly and aimlessly, in circles about the room.

"No . . . no . . . no . . . I . . . can't . . . what's happening . . . what's happening to us . . . why . . . what's happening . . . tell me . . . tell . . . me . . ."

Unnerved by her hysteria, Ben grabbed her, and shook her hard to bring her out of it—and her sobbing jerked to a halt, but she remained staring right through him—her eyes seemingly focused beyond him, at some far distant point. Her speech, still detached and rambling, became a little more coherent.

"We were in the cemetery . . . me . . . and Johnny . . . my brother, Johnny . . . we brought flowers for . . . this . . . man . . . came after me . . . and Johnny . . . he . . . he fought . . . and now he . . . he's . . ."

"All right! All right!" Ben shouted, directly into the girl's face—he had a feeling that if he couldn't bring her out of her present state of mind, she was going to go right off the deep end; she might kill herself or do something which would result in destruction for both of them. He tightened his grip on her wrists, and she wrenched against him.

"Get your hands off me!"

She flung herself away from him, beating him across the chest, taking him by surprise. But in her momentum, she stumbled over one of the table legs, barely regained her balance, and threw her body against the front door and stood there, poised as if to run out into the night.

She rambled, losing any semblance of rationality.

"We've got to help him . . . got to get Johnny . . . we've got to go out and find him . . . bring him . . ."

She advanced toward Ben, pleading with tears, the desperate tears of a frightened child.

"Bring him here . . . we'll be safe . . . we can help him . . . we . . ."

The man stepped toward her. She backed away, suddenly frightened, holding one hand toward him defensively, and the other toward her mouth. "No . . . no . . . please . . . please . . . we've got to . . . we . . ."

He took one deliberate stride toward her. "Now . . . you calm down," he said softly. "You're safe here. We can't take no chances . . ."

She pouted, and tears rolled down her cheeks.

"We've got to get Johnny," she said, weakly. And she put her fingers in her mouth and stared wide-eyed at Ben, like a small child.

"Now . . . come on, now . . . you settle down," he told her. "You don't know what these things are. It ain't no Sunday-school picnic out there . . ."

She began sobbing hysterically, violently—it was clear she had gone totally to pieces.

"Please . . . pleeeeese . . . No . . . no . . . no . . . Johnny . . . Johnny . . . pleeeese . . ."

Ben struggled to calm her, to hold her still, as she writhed and squirmed to get away from him. Despite his strength, she wrenched free—because he was trying hard not to hurt her. She stared at him, their eyes met in an instant of calm—and then she screamed and started beating at him and kicking him—kicking him again and again, while he struggled to pin her arms at her sides and hold her immobile against a wall. With brute force, he shoved her backwards finally, propelling her into a soft chair—but she sprung up again, screaming and slapping at his face. He was forced to grab her again, in a bear hug, practically slamming her into a corner. Then—he hated to do it—he brought up one powerful fist and punched her—but she jerked her head and the blow was misplaced, and did not put her out of commission. But it shocked her into dumb, wounded silence—long enough for him to hit her again, squarely. And her eyes fell sorrowfully on his and she began to crumple—she fell limp against him, as he supported her weight, easing her into his arms.

Holding her, he looked dumbly about the room. His eyes fell on the sofa. He did not carry, but almost walked her to the sofa, permitting her dead weight to fold onto it, and easing her head onto a cushion.

He stepped back and looked at her, and felt sorry for what he had to do. Still, she looked so peaceful lying there, as though she were not in any kind of danger at all. Her blonde hair was in disarray, though. And her face was wet with tears. And she was going to have a bruise where he had punched her on the chin.

Ben trembled. He hoped for both their sakes that he could find a way to pull them through. It was not going to be easy.

It was not going to be easy at all.

CHAPTER 3

Next to the couch where Barbara lay unconscious, there was a cabinet radio of the type people used to buy in the 1930's. Ben stabbed at a button, and a glow came to the yellowed dial indicator of the radio, behind its plate of old glass, and while he waited for it to warm up he looked around for the tin of nails he had given to Barbara some time ago. He found it on the floor where Barbara had dropped it, and he selected some nails and slid them into his pocket. The radio began hissing and crackling with static. He returned to it, and played with the tuning dial. At first, he could get nothing but static—then it spun past what sounded like a voice, and Ben adjusted it carefully, trying to find the spot. Finally, the tuner brought in a metallic monotone voice . . .

"... ERGENCY RADIO NETWORK. NORMAL BROADCAST FACILITIES HAVE BEEN TEMPORARILY DISCONTINUED. STAY TUNED TO THIS NETWORK FOR EMERGENCY INFORMATION. YOUR LAW ENFORCEMENT AGENCIES URGE YOU TO REMAIN IN YOUR HOMES. KEEP ALL DOORS AND WINDOWS LOCKED OR BOARDED SHUT. USE ALL FOOD, WATER, AND MEDICAL SUPPLIES SPARINGLY. CIVIL DEFENSE FORCES ARE ATTEMPTING TO GAIN CONTROL OF

THE SITUATION. STAY NEAR YOUR RADIO, AND REMAIN TUNED TO THIS FREQUENCY. DO NOT USE YOUR AUTOMOBILE. REMAIN IN YOUR HOMES. KEEP ALL DOORS AND WINDOWS LOCKED."

A long pause. A crackle. Then the message began repeating. It was a recording.

"OUR LIVE BROADCASTERS WILL CONVEY INFORMATION AS RECEIVED FROM CIVIL DEFENSE HEADQUARTERS. THIS IS YOUR CIVIL DEFENSE EMERGENCY RADIO NETWORK. NORMAL BROADCAST FACILITIES HAVE BEEN TEMPORARILY DISCONTINUED. STAY TUNED TO THIS WAVELENGTH..."

Ben waved his hand in disgust—at the repetition of the radio—and moved away as it continued its announcement. He returned to the heavy wooden table top still leaning against the wall beneath the living room window. Keeping his own body back in the shadows of the room, Ben peeled back the window curtain just enough to peer outside into the darkness of the lawn.

He saw there were now four ominous figures standing in the yard.

The metallic voice of the radio recording continued to repeat itself.

And the figures stood very still, their arms dangling, aspects of their silhouettes revealing tattered clothing or shaggy hair. They were cold, dead things.

Something in the distance suddenly startled Ben. From across the road, a figure was moving toward the house. The ghoulish beings were increasing in number, hour by hour. It was nothing that Ben had not expected, had not taken into account; still the actuality of it caused his heart to leap with fear each time he saw new evidence of it.

If the things increased sufficiently in number, it was only a matter of time before they would start to attack the house, hammering and pounding, trying to force their way in.

Ben spun away from the door and rushed to the fireplace. He reached for his matches. In a little stand by the couch where Barbara lay unconscious, there was a bunch of old magazines. Grabbing them, Ben ripped pages loose and crumpled them into the fireplace. He piled kindling wood and a few larger logs, then touched the paper with a match and watched a small fire take hold.

On the mantle was a can of charcoal-lighter. Ben grabbed it gratefully and sprayed it into the fire and it whooshed into a larger blaze, almost singeing the big man's face as he worked. The larger logs began to burn. He returned to the window.

The recorded message continued to repeat itself.

"...FORCEMENT AGENCIES URGE YOU TO REMAIN IN YOUR HOMES. KEEP ALL DOORS AND WINDOWS LOCKED OR BOARDED SHUT. USE ALL FOOD, WATER AND MEDICAL SUPPLIES SPARINGLY. CIVIL DEFENSE FORCES ARE ATTEMPTING TO..."

Ben hoisted the table top to the windowsill and struggled to brace it there while he placed a nail into position. He pounded hard with the claw hammer...driven by desperation...another nail...and another. With the table secure, he checked it hastily and rushed to another window and lifted the edge of its curtains and peered out.

Now there were five figures on the lawn.

Ben pivoted, letting the edge of the curtain drop, and rushed to the fire, where the biggest logs had now begun to blaze. He seized two of the discarded table legs, ripped curtains from the boarded-up window and used strips of the cloth to wrap around the ends of the table legs, then drenched the cloth with charcoal-lighter and plunged the table legs into the fire making two good flaming torches. A torch in each hand, he moved toward the door.

He nudged a big padded armchair ahead of him to the door and, taking both torches in one hand, pulled the curtain aside for another look at the yard.

The figures out there still stood silently, watching the house.

With charcoal-lighter, Ben drenched the padded armchair and touched it with a torch. It caught fire instantly, and the flames licked and climbed, casting flickering light throughout the house. The heat on Ben's face was severe, but he had to fight it as he lunged for the door, unbolting it and flinging it wide open.

From the doorway, the flaming chair cast eerie, irregular illumination out onto the lawn, and the waiting figures stepped back slightly, as though they were afraid.

Ben shoved the chair through the doorway and slid it across the front porch. He toppled it over the edge, and the flaming bulk tumbled down the steps onto the front lawn. In the rolling motion, flames leapt and sparks flew, and small particles of the chair's stuffing leapt and glowed in the night wind.

The bonfire raged in the tall grass.

Ben watched for a moment, as the waiting figures backed farther away.

Inside the house again, Ben banged the front door shut and fastened the bolt.

"... ORCES ARE ATTEMPTING TO GAIN CONTROL OF THE SITUATION. STAY NEAR YOUR RADIO, AND REMAIN TUNED TO THIS FREQUENCY. DO NOT USE YOUR AUTOMOBILE. REMAIN IN ..."

Hurrying to the window, Ben put more nails into the table top, fastening it securely, then he stood back and surveyed the room, his glance lingering on areas of possible vulnerability. There was the second large window, still unboarded, to the left of the door; a smaller side window; a window in the dining area on the other side of the house; and the front door, which had been bolted but not boarded up.

Ben turned, still inspecting, and his eyes suddenly grew wide.

The girl was sitting up on the couch; and it was her demeanor that had startled Ben more than the fact that she had regained consciousness. Her face was bruised, and she sat in silence staring at the floor. The radio droned on, enveloping her in its metallic repetitious tone, and the fire played on her face and reflected in her eyes . . . staring . . . and blinking very seldom.

Ben took off his sweater and moved toward her. He fixed the sweater over her shoulders and looked sympathetically into her face. She just stared at the floor. Ben felt dumb and helpless, and he was both ashamed and embarrassed by what he had done to her to end their struggle earlier, even though at the time it had been a necessary thing. For a long time, he waited for a response from the girl—perhaps an outburst of anger or resentment—but no response came. Forlornly, he moved to the pile of lumber in the center of the floor, chose a table-board, and went to the front window, which was still unboarded.

". . . BROADCASTERS WILL CONVEY INFORMATION AS RECEIVED FROM CIVIL DEFENSE HEADQUARTERS. THIS IS YOUR CIVIL DEFENSE EMERGENCY RADIO NETWORK. NORMAL BROADCAST FACILITIES HAVE BEEN . . ."

Ben succeeded in boarding up the other two windows in the living room, then moved to the front door. He got the ironing board and placed it across the door horizontally, drove nails through the board into the molding and tested it for strength; it seemed to be sufficiently strong to help keep the things out. Ben moved on in his urgency to make the house secure against attack.

In the dining area, there were two closed doors. Trying one, he found it locked, examined it, and found no latch; apparently, someone had locked it with a key. It seemed to be a closet door. Ben yanked and tugged at it several times, but it would not yield, so he concluded it was secure enough and left it alone . . . concluding that it had obviously been locked by the owner of the house, who lay dead in the hallway upstairs.

Ben found the other door unlocked, and it led into a den with several windows. Disappointed at the added vulnerability, Ben let out a long sigh, then thought for a moment, staring around the room. Finally, he exited briskly, slamming the door to the den and locking it behind him with the skeleton key protruding from its keyhole. His intention was to board the den up instead of attempting to secure the bay windows.

But the skeleton key gave him an idea, and he snatched it out of its keyhole and went to the dining room which would not open before. He jammed the key in the keyhole of the dining-room door, tried to turn it, jiggled and played with it for a while, but the door would not open. He put the key in his pocket and gave up on the door.

The supply of lumber in the center of the living room was dwindling. Ben's eyes fell momentarily on the motionless, sad figure of Barbara as he moved to check it out. She did not look back at him at all, and he bent over the pile of wood and selected another of the table-boards, for the purpose of boarding the den door. About to start hammering, a thought struck him—and he unlocked the door again and entered the room. There were chairs, a desk, a bureau... he stepped to the desk and started to rummage through the drawers. He pulled out papers, a stack of pencils and pens, a compass—a hundred little odds and ends. Another drawer, a hundred more virtually useless items... he left it hanging open. The bureau contained mostly clothing; he ripped open the big drawers, tumbling the clothing out, and hurled them through the doorway and into the dining area, with a scrape and a crash. One drawer—two—their contents spilling out onto the floor. He looked back at the bureau, and suddenly realizing a use for it, he grabbed hold of it and shoved the huge heavy piece of furniture through the doorway, walking it through the tight opening until it cleared, scraping grooves of paint out of the door-jambs. The same for the large, old-fashioned desk—which warranted another struggle, as the man attempted to secure all things of possible value before finally nailing the den door shut.

In the closet, there was a lot of old clothing; Ben found a good warm coat and jacket and flung them over his shoulder. High on the closet shelves were piles of old boxes, suitcases, hatboxes, and an old umbrella. He paused for an instant, debating their worth, or the possible worth of what they might contain. At his feet his eyes fell on still more clutter: boxes, umbrellas, dust shoes and slippers. He picked up a pair of ladies' flats and examined them, thinking of the barefoot girl out on the couch, and tucked them under his arm. As he pulled away, something caught his eye—within the dark recesses of the closet, something shiny: the sheen of a finished piece of wood, a familiar shape lying under a pile of dirty clothing. He reached out eagerly, and his hand found what he had hoped: a rifle. He set everything down and rummaged even more eagerly all over the floor of the closet—through shoe boxes, under things—items came flying out of the closet. A shoe box contained old letters and postcards. But in a cigar box, clattering around with pipe cleaners and cleaning fluid, there was a maintenance manual and a box of ammunition.

He flipped open the box, found it better than half full, and counted the cartridges—twenty-seven of them.

The rifle was a lever-action Winchester, .32 caliber. A good, powerful weapon, with plenty of impact. Ben worked the lever to clear the load—and, one after the other, seven more cartridges ejected and clattered onto the floor. He scooped them up, put them in the box with the others, and stuffed the manual into his back pocket; then, deciding to take the whole cigar box full of material, he tucked it under his arm, gathered jackets and shoes, and left the room.

In the dining room, he dropped the load of supplies on top of the drawerless bureau, and the sight of the girl in the living room stopped him short. She remained sitting as before, not moving.

Ben called out.

"We're all right, now. This place is good and solid. And I found a gun—a gun and some bullets."

He looked at Barbara from across the room. She seemed to

take no note of his talking. He turned and picked up the table-board and the hammer, to begin boarding the den, and continued talking, as if he could luck onto some words that would cause her to respond.

"So, we have a radio...and sooner or later somebody will come to get us out of here. And we have plenty of food...for a few days, at least—oh!—and I got you some shoes—we'll see in a minute if they fit—and I got some warm clothes for us..."

He got the table-board in place across the center of the den door, above the knob, and he began driving nails. His pounding and the repetition of the radio message were the only sounds. The last nail in, the check for sturdiness, and the big man turned to the girl again.

"...AGENCIES URGE YOU TO REMAIN IN YOUR HOMES. KEEP ALL DOORS AND WINDOWS..."

Other than her upright position, the girl showed no signs of life. Her wide eyes just stared at the floor, or through it, as though at some point beyond.

"...LOCKED OR BOARDED SHUT..."

"Hey, that's us—" Ben said. "Our windows are boarded up. We're doing all right—"

He managed a smile, but with the girl not looking at him his attempt was half hearted. He took up the rifle, the cigar box, a coat and the shoes he had gotten for her in one clumsy armful and knelt with his bundle in front of the girl and dropped it at her feet. Taking in his hands the shoes he had found for her, he reached out toward her and said, "These aren't the prettiest things in the world, I guess—but they ought to keep your feet warm..."

Looking up at her, he again found it hard to go on talking in the face of her catatonia. He did not really know how to cope with it. Her stillness caused him to be as gentle toward her as he could be, but she did not react, and that both puzzled and frustrated Ben.

He held one of the shoes near her foot, waiting for her to lift her leg and slip into it. Finally, taking hold of one of her ankles, he lifted it and fumbled to put the shoe on her foot. It did not go on easily, partly because it was too small, but mostly because of her limpness. But he did succeed in getting it on and he set her foot down gently and took hold of the other one.

After completing the task of putting on both her shoes for her, he leaned back on his haunches and looked into her face. She seemed to be staring at her feet.

"That's a real Cinderella story," he said, in an attempt at a joke.

No response. The man reached reflexively for his sweater pocket—but he had given Barbara his sweater.

"Hey—you know you got my cigarettes?"

He tried to smile again, but still got no reaction. He reached toward her and his hand entered the pocket of the sweater he had draped over her shoulders. His action made the girl appear to be looking directly at him, and her stare made him uncomfortable.

"You got my cigarettes," he said again, in a gentler tone, as one would try to explain some concept to a child, and as he spoke he pulled the pack of cigarettes from the pocket and leaned back on his haunches, as if he should not have ventured to touch her. He fumbled for a cigarette, put it in his mouth and lit it, trying not to look at the girl.

Her gaze still seemed to be fixed on his face.

The radio continued to drone, making her silence somehow more eerie for Ben. He would have been glad to have the metallic tones of the radio overridden by the sounds of another human voice.

"...TUNED TO THIS WAVELENGTH FOR EMERGENCY INFORMATION. YOUR LAW ENFORCEMENT AGENCIES URGE YOU TO REMAIN IN YOUR HOMES.

KEEP ALL DOORS AND WINDOWS LOCKED OR BOARDED SHUT..."

Ben inhaled his first puff of smoke and blew it through his nose. "We're doing okay," he repeated. "All our doors and windows are secure. Now...maybe you ought to lie down, you... Do you smoke?" Hopefully, he held up the burning cigarette. Her stare dropped from him back to the floor. He took another drag and blew the smoke out quickly.

"Maybe you—"

He cut himself short. He was getting nowhere. His time had better be spent in securing the old house against attack.

He scooped up the rifle and ammunition and sat in a chair across from Barbara and began methodically loading the shells into the chamber.

"Now, I don't know if you're hearing me or not—or if you're out cold or something. But I'm going upstairs now. Okay? Now we're safe down here. Nothing can get in here—at least not easy. I mean, they might be able to bust in, but it's gonna take some sweat, and I could hear them and I think I could keep them out. Later on, I'm gonna fix things good, so they can't get in nohow, but it's good for the time being. You're okay here."

He continued to load the rifle as he spoke, his cigarette dangling from his lip, causing him to squint from the smoke curling around his eyes.

"Now the upstairs is the only other way something can get in here, so I'm gonna go up and fix that."

He finished loading the last shell and was about to stand up when his glance fell on the girl again, and he tried to get through one last time.

"Okay? You gonna be all right?"

She remained silent. The man stood, tucked the rifle under his arm, grabbed up as much lumber as he could carry, and started for the stairs.

The girl looked up at him as he turned his back and he was aware of it, but he kept moving and her stare followed him.

"I'm gonna be upstairs. You're all right now. I'll be close by—upstairs. I'll come running if I hear anything."

He started up the stairs.

At the top of the landing, with a quick sucking in of his breath, he was confronted once again with the body that lay there torn and defaced. It was the corpse of a woman, probably an elderly woman, judging from the style of the remaining clothing that lay ripped into tatters and crusted in dried blood. Most of the flesh had been gnawed from the bones. The head was nearly severed from the body, the spinal column chewed through.

Ben set down his supplies and almost gagged at the sight of the corpse and tried not to look at it. The body was lying half across a blood-soaked throw rug, and a few feet away was another throw rug, with oriental patterns and a fringe sewn around its edge. The man grabbed the second rug and ripped away part of the fringe. Once the initial tear was made, the rest of the fringe peeled off easily. He freed it and, taking the rifle, tied one end of the fringe around the barrel and the other around the narrow part of the stock. This done, he slung the rifle over his shoulder, feeling more confident now that he could carry the weapon with him at all times, while he continued to work.

Then he leaned over the corpse and took hold of one end of the rug on which it lay, and began dragging it across the floor, holding his breath and gagging once or twice because of the stench of rotting flesh and the grisly appearance of the mutilated thing he had to struggle to pull down the darkened hallway, which contained several closed doors.

He deposited his ugly load at one of the doorways and threw open the door and jumped back with the rifle cocked, as if something might leap out at him. The door banged against the wall and squeaked as it settled down and stopped moving.

Nothing came out of the room.

Ben entered cautiously, with the rifle on the ready.

The room was vacant. Apparently it had been vacant for a long time. There were old yellowed newspapers on the floor, and a spider web in one corner.

There was a closet. Ben opened it slowly, pointing the rifle, ready to fire if necessary.

The closet contained nothing but dust, which rolled across the shelves in little balls and made Ben cough.

He stepped over to the windows and looked outside and down to the front lawn. Through the leafy overhang of the surrounding maple trees, he could make out the threatening forms of the dead things that stood there, watching and waiting, moving ever so slightly under the thick foliage. There appeared to be about six of them now, standing on the front lawn.

They moved around the truck, but they did not beat on it any more. Apparently they no longer felt threatened by it, now that the headlights had been smashed out. They took no more notice of it than if it had been a tree, or a pile of bricks. It seemed to have no meaning for them.

With a shudder, Ben realized that nothing human had any meaning for the dead things. Only the human beings themselves. The dead things were interested in human beings only to kill. Only to rip the flesh from their bodies. Only to make the human beings dead . . . like the dead things themselves.

Ben had a sudden impulse to smash the barrel of his rifle through the window and begin firing down on the ugly things on the lawn. But he controlled himself . . . calmed himself down. There was no sense in expending ammunition foolishly; all too well he knew how important it would be in the event of an all-out attack.

He withdrew from the window and returned to the corpse that lay at the threshold of the vacant room. Taking hold of the carpet and holding his breath once again, he dragged the corpse inside. And he left the room and shut the door, intending to board it up later. He thought of the closet door, which he could have removed and used to accomplish his boarding; but he did not think he would return for it; he did not want to enter that room ever again.

There were three more doors in the bloodstained hallway; one down at the end and two more opposite the vacant room with the corpse. The one down at the end was probably a bathroom; Ben tried it and found that it was. That left two more doors. They were probably bedrooms.

With his rifle cocked and ready to fire, Ben eased open the nearest of the two remaining doors. He jumped back, startled by his own reflection in a full-length mirror screwed onto the back of the door. His fingers groped and found the light switch. It turned out to be a child's bedroom. The bedsheets were rumpled and stained with blood, as if they had been clawed loose by someone struggling to hang on while he (or she) was being dragged from the bed. But there was no body in the room. Anxiously, afraid of what he might find, Ben searched around the bed and under it—and in the closet, which contained the clothing of a boy perhaps eleven or twelve years old. There were a couple of baseball bats, and an old skinned up baseball with the cover half off, lying on the floor of the closet.

Ben guessed that the boy was dead. Probably he had been dragged out of the house by some of those things that now stood watching and waiting outside. Probably the dead lady in the hall had been the boy's grandmother.

The thought of it renewed in Ben the terror of what was happening, which he had been able to suppress while his mind was occupied with working hard and taking defensive measures and concentrating on his own survival.

He thought of his own children—two boys, one nine and one thirteen. He did not have a wife any longer; she was dead; she had died several years ago and left him to raise the children alone. It was not easy. He loved the boys, but his job took him out of town often and much of the time he had to leave them in the care of their grandmother while he traveled and tried to earn enough money to support them all. He had been on his way home to them, but in the breakdown of communications during the present emergency his train had not arrived and he had started to hitchhike, desperate to get home. Nobody would pick him up and, walking at the outskirts of the town he had been in, he began encountering signs of destruction and murder. It puzzled him at first. He became scared. Then, in a restaurant he heard a newscast and he knew he had to get back to his family right away. He could not get a bus or cab. He even tried renting a car or just paying someone to take him where he wanted to go. Finally, hitchhiking again, a farmer picked him up and drove him a long way, but dropped him off out on the country, in the middle of nowhere it seemed. Ben got the truck on the front lawn from a dead man—a man who had been dragged from it and killed at the edge of a dirt road. He had continued listening to broadcasts on the truck radio, and he knew as much about what was happening as anyone else—which was very little. But he knew he wanted to survive and get back to his boys and their grandmother—although his reason told him that they were probably much better off in this emergency than he was himself. At least they were in a town, with other people and police protection and food and medical care if they required it. And their grandmother was a capable person. The boys would probably be all right. Ben tried to convince himself of that, but it was not easy, while he was confronted with the bloodstained sheets and mattress of the young boy who had probably been killed not so very long ago. And the old farmhouse was more a prison than it was a refuge for him and Barbara—although he did not even know her name and he could not help her, it seemed, and she was unwilling or unable to help herself.

Ben retreated from the child's room and tried the other closed door. The old lady's bedroom. He did not turn the light on at first. His eyes fell on the edge of the bed, with its white sheets, and he could see well enough to know that there were several large pieces of furniture in there. He flicked a switch, and the lights revealed nothing out of the ordinary—a bed and a couple of dressers. A quilt was folded and lying on top of the sheets, but the bed had not been slept in. Probably the old lady had gotten the boy to sleep and was preparing for bed herself when they were both attacked.

Ben entered the room and began to drag furniture out into the hallway. His plan was to get all the things of any possible use out of the boy's room and the old lady's room, and then board up the doors.

He did not know if the dead things could climb or not, or if they could think or not, or if they had any way of getting into the house through the upstairs windows. But he was not going to take any chances. Besides, when he was working, it gave him a feeling of accomplishing something and he did not worry too much or feel sorry for himself.

The noise of his work filled the old house.

Chapter 4

Downstairs, Barbara still sat dazed on the couch.

The fire flickered on her face, and the burning wood popped loudly now and again, but she did not seem to take notice of these things. Objects in the room were silhouetted and the atmosphere was stark; if earlier Barbara would have expressed some fear of such surroundings, now she did not care. Her capacity to react had been bludgeoned out of her. She was already a victim of the dead things, because they had driven her into shock—she had lost her ability to think or feel.

"...BROADCAST FACILITIES HAVE BEEN TEMPORARILY DISCONTINUED. STAY TUNED TO THIS..."

From the radio, there was suddenly a buzzing sound and crackling static. Then, a hodgepodge of newsroom sounds (as heard earlier by Barbara's brother, Johnny, on their car radio); but this time the sounds were coming in clearer: typewriters, ticker-tape machine, low voices talking in the background.

Barbara did not stir, as if she had failed to discern any difference in the broadcast, even though the repetitious Civil Defense message had ceased and something obviously was about to happen.

NIGHT OF THE LIVING DEAD

"...ER...LADIES AND GENTLEMEN...WHAT?... YEAH, YEAH...LA....YEAH, I GOT THAT ONE... WHAT?...ANOTHER ONE?...PUT IT THROUGH CENTRAL...OKAY, CHARLIE, I'M ON THE AIR NOW... YEAH. LADIES AND GENTLEMEN, LISTEN CAREFULLY, PLEASE. WE NOW HAVE THE LATEST BULLETINS FROM EMERGENCY CENTRAL..."

The voice of the newscaster sounded tired, but he began reading his report factually and unemotionally, with the air of a professional commentator who has been covering a major event for forty-eight hours and is no longer impressed with the latest developments.

"...UP-TO-THE-MINUTE REPORTS INFORM US THAT THE...SIEGE...FIRST DOCUMENTED IN THE MIDWESTERN SECTION OF THE COUNTRY IS INDEED SPREAD ACROSS THE COUNTRY, AND IS IN FACT WORLDWIDE. MEDICAL AND SCIENTIFIC ADVISORS HAVE BEEN SUMMONED TO THE WHITE HOUSE, AND REPORTERS ON THE SCENE IN WASHINGTON INFORM US THAT THE PRESIDENT IS PLANNING TO MAKE PUBLIC THE RESULTS OF THAT CONFERENCE IN AN ADDRESS TO THE NATION OVER YOUR CIVIL DEFENSE EMERGENCY NETWORK..."

None of the preceding brought any response from Barbara. She did not move. She did not get up to call Ben, in case he might hear something of value in his efforts to protect them both.

"...THE STRANGE...BEINGS...THAT HAVE APPEARED IN MOST PARTS OF THE NATION SEEM TO HAVE CERTAIN PREDICTABLE PATTERNS OF BEHAVIOR. IN THE FEW HOURS FOLLOWING INITIAL REPORTS OF VIOLENCE AND DEATH, AND APPARENTLY

DERANGED ATTACKS ON THE LIVES OF PEOPLE TAKEN COMPLETELY OFF GUARD, IT HAS BEEN ESTABLISHED THAT THE ALIEN BEINGS ARE HUMAN IN MANY PHYSICAL AND BEHAVIORAL ASPECTS. HYPOTHESES AS TO THEIR ORIGIN AND THEIR AIMS HAVE TO THIS POINT BEEN SO VARIED AND SO DIVERSE THAT WE MUST ONLY REPORT THESE FACTORS TO BE UNKNOWN. TEAMS OF SCIENTISTS AND PHYSICIANS PRESENTLY HAVE THE CORPSES OF SEVERAL OF THE AGGRESSORS, AND THESE CORPSES ARE BEING STUDIED FOR CLUES THAT MIGHT NEGATE OR CONFIRM EXISTING THEORIES. THE MOST... OVERWHELMING FACT... IS THAT THESE... BEINGS ARE INFILTRATING THROUGH URBAN AND RURAL AREAS THROUGHOUT THE NATION, IN FORCES OF VARYING NUMBER, AND IF THEY HAVE NOT AS YET EVIDENCED THEMSELVES IN YOUR AREA, PLEASE... TAKE EVERY AVAILABLE PRECAUTION. ATTACK MAY COME AT ANY TIME, IN ANY PLACE, WITHOUT WARNING. REPEATING THE IMPORTANT FACTS FROM OUR PREVIOUS REPORTS: THERE IS AN AGGRESSIVE FORCE... ARMY... OF UNEXPLAINED, UNIDENTIFIED... HUMANOID BEINGS... THAT HAS APPEARED... IN WORLDWIDE PROPORTIONS... AND THESE BEINGS ARE TOTALLY AGGRESSIVE... IRRATIONAL IN THEIR VIOLENCE. CIVIL DEFENSE EFFORTS ARE UNDERWAY, AND INVESTIGATIONS AS TO THE ORIGIN AND PURPOSE OF THE AGGRESSORS ARE BEING CONDUCTED. ALL CITIZENS ARE URGED TO TAKE UTMOST PRECAUTIONARY MEASURES TO DEFEND AGAINST THE... INSIDIOUS... ALIEN... FORCE. THEY ARE WEAK IN PHYSICAL STRENGTH, AND ARE EASILY DISTINGUISHABLE FROM HUMANS BY THEIR DEFORMED APPEARANCE. THEY ARE USUALLY UNARMED BUT APPEAR CAPABLE OF HANDLING WEAPONS. THEY

HAVE APPEARED, NOT LIKE AN ORGANIZED ARMY. NOT WITH ANY APPARENT REASON OR PLAN... INDEED, THEY SEEMED TO BE DRIVEN BY THE URGES OF ENTRANCED... OR... OR OBSESSED MINDS. THEY APPEAR TO BE TOTALLY UNTHINKING. THEY CAN... I REPEAT: THEY CAN BE STOPPED BY IMMOBILIZATION; THAT IS, BY BLINDING OR DISMEMBERING. THEY ARE, ON THE AVERAGE, WEAKER IN STRENGTH THAN AN ADULT HUMAN, BUT THEIR STRENGTH IS IN NUMBERS, IN SURPRISE, AND IN THE FACT THAT THEY ARE BEYOND OUR NORMAL REALM OF UNDERSTANDING. THEY APPEAR TO BE IRRATIONAL, NON-COMMUNICATIVE BEINGS... AND THEY ARE DEFINITELY TO BE CONSIDERED OUR ENEMIES IN WHAT WE MUST CALL A STATE OF... NATIONAL EMERGENCY. IF ENCOUNTERED, THEY ARE TO BE AVOIDED OR DESTROYED. UNDER NO CIRCUMSTANCES SHOULD YOU ALLOW YOURSELVES OR YOUR FAMILIES TO BE ALONE OR UNGUARDED WHILE THIS MENACE PREVAILS. THESE BEINGS ARE FLESH-EATERS. THEY ARE EATING THE FLESH OF THE PEOPLE THEY KILL. THE PRINCIPAL CHARACTERISTIC OF THEIR ONSLAUGHT IS THEIR DEPRAVED, INSANE QUEST FOR HUMAN FLESH. I REPEAT: THESE ALIEN BEINGS ARE EATING THE FLESH OF THEIR VICTIMS..."

At this Barbara bolted from the couch in wild, screaming hysteria, as though the words of the commentator had finally penetrated her numbed state and forced upon her brain a realization of what exactly had happened to her brother. She could hear the ripping sounds of his flesh and could see the specter of the thing that had killed him, and her screams struggled to obliterate these things as she hurtled across the room and crashed her body against the front door.

Startled, unslinging his gun, Ben leaped down the stairs. The girl was clawing at the barricades, trying to break out of the house, sobbing in wild desperation. Ben rushed toward her, but she writhed out of his reach, ran across the room—toward the maze of heaped-up furniture in front of the door in the dining area which Ben had found locked.

Suddenly that door flew open and—from out of the maze of furniture—strong hands grabbed Barbara. She screamed in terror, as Ben leaped and began swinging the butt of his rifle.

Whoever it was who had gotten hold of Barbara, he let go of the girl and ducked, and the rifle butt missed him and crashed against a piece of furniture. Quickly, Ben brought it up, and almost squeezed the trigger.

"No! Don't shoot!" a voice yelled, and Ben narrowly stopped himself from firing.

"We're from town—we're not—" the man said.

"We're not some of those things!" a second voice said, and Ben saw another man step out from behind the partially opened door, which he had thought to be locked.

The man hiding behind the furniture stood up, slowly as though he thought Ben might still shoot him. He was not a full-grown man. He was a boy, maybe sixteen years old, in blue jeans and denim jacket. The man behind him was about forty years old, bald, wearing a white shirt and loosened tie—and carrying a heavy pipe in his hand.

"We're not some of those things," the bald man repeated. "We're in the same fix you're in."

Barbara had flung herself onto the couch, and was sobbing sporadically. All three men glanced at her, as though she were an object of common concern that would convince each of them of the other's good intentions. The boy finally went over to her and looked at her sympathetically.

Ben stared, dumbfounded at the presence of the strangers.

The radio voice continued with its information about the emergency.

The bald man backed away from Ben nervously, not taking his

eyes off of Ben's rifle, and crouched beside the radio to listen, still holding his length of pipe.

"... PERIODIC REPORTS, AS INFORMATION REACHES THIS NEWSROOM, AS WELL AS SURVIVAL INFORMATION AND A LISTING OF RED CROSS RESCUE POINTS, WHERE PICK-UPS WILL BE MADE AS OFTEN AS POSSIBLE WITH THE EQUIPMENT AND STAFF PRESENTLY AVAILABLE..."

Ben still stood staring at the two new people. He exuded, despite himself, an air of resentment, as though they had intruded on his private little fortress. He did not resent their presence as much as he resented the fact that they had obviously been in the house all this time without coming up to help him or Barbara. He was not sure of their motive in revealing themselves now, and he did not know how completely he should trust them.

The bald man looked up from the radio. "There's no need to stare at us that way," he said to Ben.

"We're not dead, like those things out there. My name is Harry Cooper. The boy's name is Tom. We've been holed up in the cellar."

"Man, I could've used some help," Ben said, barely controlling his anger. "How long you guys been down there?"

"That's the cellar. It's the safest place," Harry Cooper said, with a tone in his voice to convey the idea that anybody who wouldn't hole up in the cellar in such an emergency must be an idiot.

The boy, Tom, got up from beside the couch, where he had been trying to think of a way to comfort Barbara, and came over to join in the ensuing discussion.

"Looks like you got things pretty secure up here," Tom said to Ben, in a friendly way.

Ben pounced on him.

"Man, you mean you couldn't hear the racket we were making up here?"

Cooper pulled himself to his feet. "How were we supposed to know what was going on?" he said, defensively. "It could have been those things trying to get in here, for all we knew."

"That girl was screaming," Ben said, angrily. "Surely you must know what a girl's screaming sounds like. Those things don't make that kind of noise. Anybody decent would know somebody was up here that could use some help."

Tom said, "You can't really tell what's going on from down there. The walls are thick. You can't hear."

"We thought we could hear screams," Cooper added. "But that might have meant those things were in the house after her."

"And you wouldn't come up and help?" Ben turned his back on them, contemptuously.

The boy seemed to be ashamed of himself, but Cooper remained undaunted by Ben's contempt, probably accustomed to a lifetime of rationalizing his cowardice.

"Well...I...if...there was more of us..." the boy said. But he turned away, and did not have the gumption to continue his excuses.

Cooper persisted.

"That racket sounded like the place was being ripped apart. How were we supposed—"

But Ben cut him off.

"You just said it was hard to hear down there. Now you say it sounded like the place was being ripped apart. You'd better get your story straight, mister."

Cooper exploded.

"Bullshit! I don't have to take any crap from you. Or any insults. We've got a safe place in that cellar. And you or nobody else is going to tell me to risk my life when I've got a safe place."

"All right...why don't we settle—" Tom began. But Cooper did not allow him to continue. He went on talking, but in a calmer voice, espousing his own point of view.

"All right. We came up. Okay? We're here. Now I suggest we

all go back downstairs before any of these things find out we're in here."

"They can't get in here," Ben said, as though it were a certainty. He had plenty of doubts in his own mind, but he did not feel like discussing them for the benefit of those two strangers who were, as far as he could see, one boy and one coward.

"You got the whole place boarded up?" Tom asked. He was a bit skeptical, but he was willing to submerge his skepticism in favor of group harmony.

"Most of it," Ben replied, keeping his voice in an even, analytical tone. "All but the upstairs. It's weak in places, but it won't be hard to fix it up good. I got the stuff and I—"

Cooper broke in, his voice at a high pitch again.

"You're insane! You can't make it secure up here. The cellar's the safest place in the damned house!"

"I'm tellin' you they can't get in here." Ben shouted at him.

"And I'm telling you those things turned over our car! We were damned lucky to get away in one piece—now you're trying to tell me they can't get through a lousy pile of wood?"

Ben stared for a moment, and did not know what to say. He knew the cellar had certain advantages, but he could not abide being told about it by someone like Cooper, who was obviously a coward. Ben knew he had managed to do pretty well so far, and he did not want to throw in his lot entirely with someone who might panic or run, in an emergency.

Tom took advantage of the lull to throw in an additional fact, which he thought might soften Ben and stop the argument between him and Cooper:

"Harry's wife and kid are downstairs. The kid's been hurt, pretty badly. Harry doesn't want to leave them anywhere where they might be threatened, or subjected to any more attacks by those things."

The statement took Ben by surprise. He softened, and exhaled a deep breath. Nobody said anything for a long moment, until finally he swallowed, and made his point again.

"Well . . . I . . . I think we're better off up here."

Glancing around at the barricades, Tom said, "We could strengthen all this stuff up, Mr. Cooper." And he eyed the bald man hopefully, looking to him to cooperate with Ben at least a little, so that they might be safer and make the best of the circumstances.

Ben continued, emphasizing the strong points of his argument. "With all of us working, we can fix this place up so nothing can get in here. And we have food. The stove. The refrigerator. A warm fire. And we have the radio."

Cooper merely glowered, in a new burst of anger. "Man, you're crazy. Everything that's up here, we can bring downstairs with us. You've got a million windows up here. All these windows—you're gonna make them strong enough to keep those things out?"

"Those things don't have any strength," Ben said, with controlled anger. "I smashed three of them and pushed another one out the door."

"I'm telling you they turned our car over on its roof!" Cooper spat.

"Oh, hell, any good five men can do that," Ben said.

"That's my point! Only there's not going to be five—there's going to be twenty...thirty...maybe a hundred of those things! Once they all know we're in here, this place will be crawling with them!"

Calmly, Ben said, "Well, if there's that many, they're gonna get us no matter where we are."

"We fixed the cellar door so it locks and boards from the inside," Tom said. "It's really strong. I don't think anything could get in there."

"It'd be the only door we'd have to protect," Cooper added, in a slightly less hysterical tone. "But all these doors and windows—why, we'd never know where they were going to hit us next."

"But the cellar has one big disadvantage," Tom pointed out. "There's no place to run—I mean, if they ever did get in—there's no back exit. We'd be done for."

The bald man stared, his mouth wide open. He could not believe Tom would desert the sanctity of the basement, for any reason, because he himself felt so driven to remain there, as if nothing could touch him—like a rat in his hole.

"I think we should fortify the entire house as good as we can—and keep the basement for a stronghold, a last resort," Ben said, decisively. "That way we can run to the cellar when everything else falls through. We can maintain contact with what's going on out there for as long as possible."

"That makes sense," Tom said. "I don't know, Mr. Cooper. I think he's right. I think we should stay up here."

"The upstairs is just as much of a trap as the basement," Ben said, analytically. "There are three rooms up there and they have to be boarded up. But those things are weak. We can keep them out. I have this gun now, and I didn't have it before and I still managed to beat three of them off. Now . . . we might have to try and get out of here on our own, because there's no guarantee anyone is going to send help—and maybe nobody even knows we're in here. If someone does come to help—and this house gets full of those things—we'd be scared to open the cellar door and let the rescue party know we're in here."

"How many of the things are outside now?" Tom asked.

"I think six or seven," Ben replied. "I can't get an accurate count because of the darkness and the trees."

"Look, you two can do whatever you like," Cooper said, morosely. "I'm going back down to the cellar, and you'd better decide—because I'm gonna board up that door and I'm not gonna be crazy enough to unlock it again, no matter what happens."

"Wait a minute!" Tom exclaimed. "Let's think about this for a minute, Mr. Cooper—all our lives depend on what we decide."

"Nope. I've made my decision. You make yours. And you can stew in your own juice if you decide to stay up here."

Alarmed, Tom began to urge desperately. "Now wait a minute, damn it, let's think about this a while—we can make it to the cellar if we have to—and if we do decide to stay down there, we'll need some things from up here. Now, let's at least consider this a while—"

Ben added: "Man, if you box yourself into that cellar, and if there's a lot of those things that get into the house—you've had it. At least up here you can make a break for it—you outran them once, or you wouldn't even be here."

Flustered and still not quite decided, Tom went to one of the front windows and peered out through the barricade.

"Yeah, looks like six—or maybe eight of them out there now," he said, his voice showing his increased alarm after attempting a head-count.

"That's more than there were," Ben admitted. "There are quite a few out back, too—unless they're the same ones that are out here now."

He burst into the kitchen, as the fringed rifle sling snapped and the weapon started to fall; he twisted to keep it on his back and tried to grab it, reaching behind. His attention on the gun, he did not see the window as he moved toward it; but regaining control of the gun he looked up—and stopped cold. Hands were reaching through broken glass behind the barricades—graying, rotting hands, scratching, reaching, trying to grab—and through aspects of the glass could be seen the inhuman faces behind the hands. The barrier was being strained, no doubt about that, but it seemed to be holding well enough.

The man smashed with the rifle butt against the ugly extremities. Once. Twice. The rifle butt stamped down on the decaying hands... driving one of them back with a shattering of the already broken glass it had been reaching through. The rifle butt smashed another of the hands against the window molding solidly—but the hand, unfeeling of any pain, continued to claw after a hold.

Ben slid his finger to the trigger and turned the rifle, smashing the barrel through some unbroken glass, and two of the gray hands seized the protruding metal. A dead face appeared behind the hands... ugly... expressionless... rotting flesh hanging from the bones. Ben's face looked directly through the opening in the barricade into the dead eyes beyond, the man struggling desperately to control the weapon and the zombie thing outside trying to pull it away by the barrel. For a brief instant, the muzzle pointed directly at the hideous face; then . . . BLAM! The report shattered the air and the lifeless thing was thrown back, propelled by the blast, its head torn partially away, its still outstretched hands falling back with the crumpling body.

The other hands continued to clutch and grab.

Tom rushed into the kitchen behind Ben, and Harry was standing cautiously a few feet from the doorway. A distant voice, that of Harry's wife, Helen, suddenly began to cry out from the cellar.

"Harry! Harry! Harry! are you all right?!"

"It's all right, Helen. We're all right!" Cooper called out in a quavering voice which betrayed his fear and anxiety and was not likely to calm Helen very much.

Tom immediately rushed to Ben's aid. The big man was pounding at a dead hand that was trying to work at the barricade from the bottom. The blows from the rifle butt seemed ineffectual as the hand, oblivious except for the physical jouncing from the impact, continued to claw and grab. Tom leaped against the barricaded window and seized the rotting wrist with both his hands and tried to bend the wrist back in an effort to break it, but it seemed limp and almost totally pliable. Disgust crept over Tom's face. He tried to scrape the cold thing against the edge of the broken glass, and the absence of blood was immediately evident in an appalling way, as the sharp edge of broken glass ripped into what looked like rotting flesh. Another hand suddenly grabbed at Tom's hand and tried to pull it through the glass. Tom yelled, and Ben tried to swing the barrel of his rifle toward the thing struggling with Tom; but another hand clutched at him even while he was trying to help the boy—a hand was clawing and ripping Ben's shirt, but he managed to free himself and step back long enough to aim the gun. Another loud blast, and the hands Tom was fighting jerked back and fell into darkness. Badly shaken, Tom just stared through an opening in the broken glass behind the barricade. Ben took careful aim and pulled the trigger again; the blast ripped through the thing's chest, leaving a big gaping hole—but it remained on its feet, backing slowly away.

"Oh, good God!" Tom exclaimed, panicked at the failure of the rifle, as the dead thing recovered and stepped forward again, oblivious to the fact that half of its upper torso had been blown away.

Ben cocked his weapon and fired again—another loud report. This time the shell ripped through the thing's thigh, just below the pelvis. The thing backed away, but as it tried to put weight on its right leg it fell to a heap. Tom and Ben just stared, in disbelief. The thing was still moving away, dragging itself with its arms and pushing against the ground with its remaining useful leg.

"Mother of God! What are these things?"

Tom fell back against the wall. His eyes fell on Harry, and he saw the unmistakable cowardly fear in the bald man's face.

Ben wet his lips, took a deep breath and held it, carefully sighting down the barrel of the rifle again. He pulled the trigger. The shell seemed to blow open the skull of the crawling form, and it fell backwards.

"Damn . . . damn thing from hell!"

Ben's voice trembled as he let out his held breath.

Outside, the thing that had fallen limply, without the use of its eyes, moved its arms in groping, clutching motions, seemingly still trying to drag itself away.

From the cellar:

"Harry! Harry!"

After a moment of silence, Ben turned from the barricaded window with its shattered glass. "We have to board up this place a lot stronger," he said and, out of breath, he made a move to start to work when Harry spoke: "You're crazy! Those things are gonna be at every door and window in this place! We've got to get into the cellar!"

Ben turned to Harry and faced him, with absolute fury in his eyes. In his rage, his voice bellowed, deeper and more commanding.

"Get into your goddamned cellar! Get the hell out of here!"

The shouting stopped Harry for an instant, then his adamancy returned. His mind made up, he knew he would have to go into the cellar without the others if need be, and he had better gather whatever supplies they would let him keep without interference. Perhaps in the confusion of the moment, he thought, he could snatch up a lot of things without an argument. He moved toward the refrigerator, but Ben stopped him.

"Don't you touch any of that food," Ben warned

He tightened his grip on the rifle, and though he did not point it at Harry, Harry was well aware of the power it implied.

Harry allowed his fingers to fall away from the handle of the refrigerator.

"Now, if I stay up here," Ben said, "I'm gonna be fighting for what's up here—and that food and that radio and anything else that's up here is part of what I'm fighting for. And you are dead wrong—you understand? But if you're going to the cellar, get your ass moving—go down there and get out of here, man, and don't mess with me anymore."

Harry turned to Tom.

"This man is crazy, Tom! He's crazy! We've got to have food down there! We've got a right!"

Ben confronted Tom also. "You going down there with him?"

"No beating around the bush. You going, or ain't you? This is your last chance."

After a long moment of silence, Tom turned and faced Harry Cooper apologetically, for he had decided in favor of Ben.

"Harry . . . I think he's right . . ."

"You're crazy."

"I really think we're better off up here."

"You're crazy. I have a kid down there. She couldn't possibly take all the racket up here, and those things reaching through the glass. We'll be lucky if she lives, as it is now."

"Okay," Ben said. "You're the kid's father. If you're dumb enough to go die in that trap, it's your business. But I'm not dumb enough to go with you. It's just bad luck for the kid that her old man's so dumb. Now, you get the hell down the cellar. You can be boss down there. And I'm boss up here. And you ain't taking any of this food, and you ain't touching anything that's up here."

"Harry, we can get food to you," Tom said, "if you want to stay down there and . . ."

"You bastards!" Harry said. From the cellar, his wife was still crying out:

"Harry! Harry! What's going on, Harry?"

He moved toward the cellar, but Tom stopped him.

"Send Judy up here," Tom said. "She'll want to stay up here with me."

Ben glanced at Tom, with a surprised expression on his face. No one had told him there was anybody in the cellar except for Harry's wife and daughter.

"My girlfriend," Tom explained. "Judy's my girlfriend."

"You should've told me she was down there," Ben said.

In the meantime, Harry had pivoted and stomped down the cellar stairs, and the sound of lighter footsteps told them the girl was on her way up.

She hugged Tom and looked sheepishly at Ben. She was about Tom's age, dressed similarly to him, in blue jeans and denim jacket. She was a pretty girl, blond, scared, and probably—Ben thought—going to be about as much of a problem as Barbara. With Tom, she moved to the closed cellar door, behind which could be heard the sounds of Harry boarding it up.

"You know I won't open this door again!" Harry shouted, through it. "I mean it!"

"We can fix it up here!" Tom shouted back, not giving up. "With your help we could—"

"Let him go," Ben said. "His mind is made up. You'd be better off to just forget about him."

"We'd be better off up here!" Tom shouted. "There are good places we can run to up here!"

From behind the cellar door, there was no reply. Just the sound of Harry's footsteps going down the stairs.

Ben tied the broken fringe back onto the rifle, then began reloading it, replacing the spent shells. When it was loaded, he strapped it to his shoulder again, then turned and moved toward the upstairs. In passing, his glance fell on Barbara; he stepped backwards off the stairs and looked at her.

The radio had taken up again with its monotonous recorded message.

Tom had not given up and was still pleading with Harry, shouting against the closed cellar door.

"Harry, we'd be better off if we was all working together! We'll let you have food when you need it—" He glanced warily at Ben, half-expecting reprisal for making his offer of food, contrary to Ben's wishes. "And if we pound on the door, those things might be chasing us, and you can let us in."

Still no answer from Harry.

Tom listened a while longer, then retreated, disappointed and worried about the fractionalization that had occurred and the realization that each of them could be heavily dependent on any of the others if worse came to worst.

Judy was sitting quietly in a chair, and she gave Tom a worried look as he stood beside her and brushed her cheek with his hand.

Ben was with Barbara, stooping beside her as she lay on the couch. She stared into an unseeing void. Ben felt sorry for her, and just as helpless as ever where she was concerned.

"Hey . . . hey, honey?"

She made no response. He brushed her hair back from her eyes. She trembled; it almost seemed for a moment that she might acknowledge his tenderness, but she did not. Ben felt very sorrowful, almost as he would feel for one of his children at a time of illness. He massaged his forehead and eyes, tired from the fear and exertion of the past hours. He bent finally to cover the girl with a coat that he had brought from the den, then stepped away and heaved a log onto the fire and stirred it to keep the blaze good and warm; his primary concern in this effort was for the girl. Behind him, Tom stepped forward, and Ben sensed his presence and his worries concerning Harry Cooper.

"He's wrong, man," Ben said, positively.

Tom remained silent.

"I'm not boxing myself in down there," Ben added. "We might be here several days. We'll get it good and strong up here, and he'll come up and join us. He won't stay down there very long. He'll want to see what's going on—or maybe if we get a chance to get out, he'll come up and help us. I have a truck outside . . . but I need gas. If I could get to those pumps out back . . . maybe we'd have a chance to save ourselves."

With that, Ben turned and mounted the stairs to continue his work up there, taking it for granted that Tom would be willing and able to man the downstairs.

Chapter 5

The cellar, with its stark gray walls and dusty clutter, was cold and damp. Cardboard cartons tied with cord and a hanging grid of pipe-work all looked dirty in the heavy shadows cast by bare light bulbs. The cartons took up much of the space; they varied in size from grocery boxes with faded brand names to large packing crates that might have contained furniture. The washing machine, an old roller type, sat off in a corner of the cellar near a makeshift shower stall. Lines for drying clothes were strung over the pipe work so low that Harry was forced to duck under them as he walked from the stairs to the other side of the confining quarters.

A pair of stationary tubs and an old metallic cabinet stood against one of the walls, where Harry's wife, Helen, leaned over the faucet of one of the tubs, wetting a cloth with cold water. She looked up as Harry entered, but remained more interested in what she was doing at the moment; she wrung out the cloth, feeling it to ascertain that it retained the correct amount of dampness, and took it to where a young girl, their daughter, lay motionless atop a homemade worktable. On a pegboard above the table there were hanging tools and cables, and built into the table itself were drawers for smaller tools—screws and bolts, washers, and so forth.

Helen's movements were a little stiff in the coolness of the cellar; she was wearing a dress and sweater while a warmer coat was spread on the table under the little girl, its sides flopped up and over her, covering her legs and chest. The woman bent over her daughter and wiped her head with the cool cloth.

Harry quietly walked up behind Helen as she concentrated on caring for the girl, pulling the coat more securely around her. Without bothering to look up at Harry, she said, "Karen has a bad fever now."

Harry sighed, with concern for his daughter. Then he said, "There's two more people upstairs."

"Two?"

"Yeah," Harry acknowledged. Then, half-defensively: "I wasn't about to take any unnecessary chances."

Helen remained silent, while Harry awaited some sign that she approved of his decision. "How did we know what was going on up there?" he said finally, flinging his arms into the air with a shrug. Then he reached nervously to his breast pocket for a cigarette, produced a pack that turned out to be empty, and crumpled it in his hand and pitched it to the floor. He stepped over to the worktable where there was another pack, snatched it up, and it, too, was empty—and with the same crumpling action Harry discarded the pack, violently this time, the action spinning him into a position facing his wife and daughter. Helen continued to quietly swab the girl's forehead, while Harry stared at them for a moment.

"Does she seem to be all right?" Harry asked, anxiously.

Helen was silent. The daughter, Karen, motionless.

Harry was sweating to the point where beads of sweat had formed all over his face. He waited and, seeing no answer forthcoming, changed the subject.

"They're all staying upstairs ... idiots! We should stick together. It's the safest down here."

He went to his wife's purse and rummaged through the contents long enough to find a pack of cigarettes. He tore the pack open, yanked a cigarette out, lit it, and dragged in the first puff deeply; it made him cough slightly.

"They don't stand a chance up there. They can't hold those things off forever. There's too many ways they can get into the house up there."

Helen remained silent, as if her respect and tolerance of her husband's ideas had long ago been dissipated.

On the floor, next to the workbench, was a small transistor radio. Harry's glance fell on it and he stabbed at it, scooped it up, and clicked it on.

"They had a radio on upstairs. Must've been Civil Defense or . . . I think it's not just us, this thing is happening all over."

The tiny radio would pick up nothing but static, try as Harry might. He spun the tuning dial back and forth, listening anxiously, but across the receiving band the transistor just continued to hiss. Harry held it up and turned it into various positions, trying for reception, spinning the tuner constantly. Still, nothing but hissing. He began pacing the room, holding the radio up and down and sideways, with no results.

"This damned thing—"

Still just static.

Helen stopped wiping her daughter's forehead, neatly folded the cloth, and draped it over the prostrate girl's brow. Gently placing her hand on her daughter's chest, she looked over toward her husband, who was still pacing around the cellar, his cigarette dangling from his lip, waving the little radio around in the air.

The radio continued to emit nothing but static at varying volumes.

"Harry—"

He continued his fidgeting with the radio, as though it had become an obsession. He moved near the wall at the foot of the stairs, holding it high and still spinning the dial. He was breathing and perspiring heavily.

"Harry—that thing can't pick up anything in this stinking dungeon!"

Her rising tone of voice stopped him; he turned and looked at her; about to cry, she brought her hands up to her face. Then, shaking her head, she bit her lip and just stared at the floor.

Looking at her, Harry's anger rose and swept over him, putting him momentarily at a loss for words; his face began twitching, his emotion searching for some vehicle of expression, until he pivoted violently and flung the radio across the room, smashing it against the wall, and launched into an orgy of shouting.

"I hate you—right? I hate the kid? I wanna see you die here, right? In this stinking place! My God, Helen, do you realize what's happening? Those things are all over the place—they'll kill us all! I enjoy watching my kid suffer like this? I enjoy seeing all this happen?"

Helen's head jerked toward him. She looked at him with an expression that was half anguish and half pleading.

"Karen needs help, Harry...she needs a doctor. She's...she's going to maybe die here. We have to get out of here, Harry. We have to."

"Oh, yeah—let's just walk out. We can pack up right now and get ready to go, and I'll just say to those things—excuse me, my wife and kid are uncomfortable here, we're going into town. For God's sake...there's maybe twenty of those things out there. And there's more every minute."

Harry's sarcasm did not help him to make his point with Helen; rather, it increased her disgust with him and made her more bitter. But she knew shouting back at him would do no good. Attempting to reason with him was the only thing that ever stood a chance of changing his mind, once he had convinced himself of something—provided you could convince him that he had thought up the new idea himself, giving him the opportunity of backing off from his previous position gracefully.

"There's people upstairs," Helen said. "We should stick together, you said it yourself. Those people aren't our enemies, are they? Upstairs, downstairs—what's the difference? Maybe they can help us. Let's get out of here..."

A pounding sound interrupted her.

Both she and Harry held their breath and listened. The sound repeated itself—coming from the door at the top of the stairs. They glanced anxiously at their helpless daughter. For a long moment, they were half convinced they were being attacked. But then they heard Tom's voice.

"Harry!"

More pounding. Harry just stared up at the door and did not answer the call. He was sticking to his decision not to open the door again or have anything to do with the people upstairs. Tears welled in Helen's eyes as her frustration and disappointment in her husband increased and swept over her. More pounding. Helen looked at Harry. She knew he was a coward. More pounding; then a pause; maybe Tom was going to give up. Helen leaped up and ran to the foot of the stairs.

"Yes... yes, Tom!"

Harry, running after her, grabbed her shoulders from behind and stopped her. She squirmed and struggled to free herself.

"Harry! Let me go! Let me go!"

She struggled violently, and the force of her determination rather than her physical strength shocked Harry and cowed him, and he stepped away from her and just stared—his wife had never defied him openly like this before.

Tom's voice again sounded through the barricaded door:

"Harry... Helen... we have food, and some medicine and other things up here..."

Harry stared up at the door, speechlessly.

"There's gonna be a thing on the radio in ten minutes, Harry—a Civil Defense thing—to tell us what to do!"

Looking up at the door, Helen shouted, "We're coming up Tom! We'll be up in a minute!"

Harry spun and glowered at her.

"You're out of your mind, Helen. All it takes is a minute for those things to grab a hold of you and kill you. If they get in up there, it'll be too late to change your mind don't you see that? Can't you see that we're safe as long as we keep that door sealed up?"

"I don't give a damn!" she spat at him. "I don't care Harry—I don't care any more; I want to get out of here—go upstairs—see if someone will help us. Maybe Karen will be okay."

Calming suddenly, she stopped shouting, got control of herself, and stepped toward Harry and spoke in a softer tone.

"Harry... please... for just a minute, we'll go up and see what's up there. We'll hear the radio, and maybe we can figure some way to get out of here. Maybe with all of us we can make it, Harry."

Harry, his adamancy weakening somewhat, took the cigarette from his mouth, exhaling the last puff, and dropped it to the floor. He stepped on it to snuff it out; the smoke came in a long stream through his pursed lips.

Startlingly, Tom's voice penetrated again.

"Harry! Hey, Harry! Ben found a television upstairs! Come on up—we'll see the Civil Defense broadcast on TV."

Harry wavered. Helen spoke soothingly to him, her tone an attempt to relieve the distress she thought he must feel in going against his original decision. "Come on... let's go up. There'll be something on TV that tells us what to do. You can tell them it was me that wanted to go up."

"All right," Harry said. "All right. This is your decision. We'll go up—but don't blame me if we all get killed."

Her eyes fell away from him, and she began mounting the stairs, taking the lead as he fell in behind, so the people upstairs would know their coming up was her doing.

Together, she and Harry began unboarding the cellar door.

Chapter 6

Harry lifted the last heavy timber away, and the door came away from the jamb with a creaking noise. Helen peered out into the dining area, and beyond that into the semi-darkened living room. Harry, standing behind his wife, felt tense and hostile—and angry with himself because he had reneged on his decision about the cellar. Helen, too, was overwrought, because of the emotional strain of her argument with Harry and the fact that she was about to meet strange people in an anxious circumstance.

But only Tom and Barbara were in the living room. Barbara, overcome with nervous exhaustion and shock, was sleeping fitfully on the couch, in front of the fire.

In an effort to be friendly, Tom said, "We can see the broadcast, I think—if the TV works. I have to go help Ben carry it downstairs. Judy is in the kitchen, I'll get her, and she can take care of Karen for you while you're up here watching the television."

Helen managed a smile to express her thanks, and Tom immediately turned on his heels and went into the kitchen to get his girlfriend.

Helen moved over to the fire, seeking its warmth and looked down at Barbara sympathetically and brushed back her hair and pulled the overcoat around her shoulders.

"Poor thing... she must have been through a lot," Helen said, to no one in particular.

Harry, during these moments, had been flitting all over the house, from door to window to kitchen to living room, checking out the actual degree of security, which he felt was practically non-existent, and worrying about the imminence of attack at any second.

Tom and Judy came out of the kitchen, and Tom said to Helen, "I think her brother was killed out there." And he nodded his head toward Barbara, who moaned softly in her fitful sleep, as though she had heard his comment.

Ben came to the top of the stairs, and began shouting.

"Tom! Hey, Tom! Are you gonna give me a hand with this thing, or ain't you?"

Tom, startled, aware of his procrastination, bolted for the upstairs to help Ben while Judy opened the cellar door and went down to watch Karen.

Harry, still pacing around in his anxiety, strode briskly over to where his wife was looking after Barbara.

"Her brother was killed," Helen said, as if telling that to Harry might soften him and jolt him out of his self-interest.

"This place is ridiculous," Harry said. "There's a million weak spots up here."

Frightened suddenly by a noise, Harry paused in his pacing long enough to listen and ascertain to his satisfaction that it was only Tom and Ben, struggling with the television, making their way down the steps.

Helen glowered at Harry. "You're a pain in the ass," she told him. "Why can't you make the best of things and do something to help somebody—instead of complaining all the time?"

Harry, not really hearing her, was staring through a slat in the barricaded front window into the gloom outside.

"I can't see a damn thing out there!" he exclaimed. "There could be fifty million of those things. I can't see a thing—that's how much good these windows do us!"

Ben, who with Tom had reached the landing with the heavy

television set, arrived in time to hear the last part of Harry's remark; he glowered even as he moved with his end of the burden, but said nothing, as he and Tom dragged two chairs together and gingerly deposited the TV on them, in the center of the room. They hunted for an outlet, found it, then slid and walked the set on the two chairs until the cord was close enough to be plugged in.

As Ben knelt behind the set to plug in the cord, Harry said, "Wake that girl up. If there's going to be a thing on the tube, she might as well know where she stands. I don't want to be responsible for her."

Shocked, Helen blurted, "Harry, stop acting like a child!"

Ben got to his feet, his eyes flashing anger. "I don't want to hear any more from you, mister. If you stay up, here, you'll take your orders from me—and that includes leaving that girl alone. She needs rest—she's just about out of her head as it is now. Now, we're just going to let her sleep it off. And nobody's going to touch her unless I say so."

Ben stared Harry down for a moment, to ascertain that he had been at least temporarily squelched; then his hand plunged immediately to the television set. As he snapped it on, the occupants of the room jockeyed for vantage points in front of it, and there were a few baited seconds of dead silence as they all waited to see if the set would actually warm up. All eyes were on the tube. A hiss began, and increased in volume. Ben twisted the volume all the way. A glowing band appeared and spread, filling the screen.

"It's on! It's on!" Helen shouted.

There were murmurs of excitement and anticipation—but the tube showed nothing. No picture, no sound. Just the glow and hiss of the tube. Ben's hand raced the tuning dial through the clicks of the various stations.

Harry jumped up, fidgeting. "Play with the rabbit ears. We should be able to get something—"

Ben fussed with horizontal and vertical, with brightness and contrast. On one station, he finally got sound: he adjusted the volume. The picture tumbled; he played with it and finally brought it in. Full-screen was a commentator, in the middle of a news report.

Hushed, the people in the room settled back to watch and listen.

"... ASSIGN LITTLE CREDIBILITY TO THE THEORY THAT THIS ONSLAUGHT IS A PRODUCT OF MASS HYSTERIA..."

"Mass hysteria!" Harry snarled. "What do they think—we're imagining all this?"

"Shut up!" Ben bellowed. "I want to hear what's going on!"

"...AUTHORITIES ADVISE UTMOST CAUTION UNTIL THE MENACE CAN BE BROUGHT UNDER ABSOLUTE CONTROL. EYEWITNESS ACCOUNTS HAVE BEEN INVESTIGATED AND DOCUMENTED. CORPSES OF VANQUISHED AGGRESSORS ARE PRESENTLY BEING EXAMINED BY MEDICAL PATHOLOGISTS, BUT AUTOPSY EFFORTS HAVE BEEN HAMPERED BY THE MUTILATED CONDITION OF THESE CORPSES. SECURITY MEASURES INSTITUTED IN METROPOLITAN AREAS INCLUDE ENFORCED CURFEWS AND SAFETY PATROLS BY ARMED PERSONNEL. CITIZENS ARE URGED TO REMAIN IN THEIR HOMES. THOSE WHO IGNORE THIS WARNING EXPOSE THEMSELVES TO INTENSE DANGER—FROM THE AGGRESSORS THEMSELVES, AND FROM ARMED CITIZENRY WHOSE IMPULSE MAY BE TO SHOOT FIRST AND ASK QUESTIONS LATER. RURAL OR OTHERWISE ISOLATED DWELLINGS HAVE MOST FREQUENTLY BEEN THE OBJECTIVE OF FRENZIED, CONCERTED ATTACK. ISOLATED FAMILIES ARE IN EXTREME DANGER. ESCAPE ATTEMPTS SHOULD BE MADE IN HEAVILY ARMED GROUPS, AND BY MOTOR VEHICLE IF POSSIBLE. APPRAISE YOUR

SITUATION CAREFULLY BEFORE DECIDING ON AN ESCAPE TACTIC. FIRE IS AN EFFECTIVE WEAPON. THESE BEINGS ARE HIGHLY FLAMMABLE. ESCAPE GROUPS SHOULD STRIKE OUT FOR THE NEAREST URBAN COMMUNITY. MANNED DEFENSE OUTPOSTS HAVE BEEN ESTABLISHED ON MAJOR ARTERIES LEADING INTO ALL COMMUNITIES. THESE OUTPOSTS ARE EQUIPPED TO DEFEND REFUGEES AND TO OFFER MEDICAL AND SURGICAL ASSISTANCE. POLICE AND VIGILANTE PATROLS ARE IN THE PROCESS OF COMBING REMOTE AREAS IN SEARCH AND DESTROY MISSIONS AGAINST ALL AGGRESSORS. THESE PATROLS ARE ATTEMPTING TO EVACUATE ISOLATED FAMILIES. BUT RESCUE EFFORTS ARE PROCEEDING SLOWLY, DUE TO THE INCREASED DANGER OF NIGHT AND THE SHEER ENORMITY OF THE TASK. RESCUE, FOR THOSE IN ISOLATED CIRCUMSTANCES, IS HIGHLY UNDEPENDABLE. YOU SHOULD NOT WAIT FOR A RESCUE PARTY UNLESS THERE IS NO POSSIBILITY OF ESCAPE. IF YOU ARE FEW AGAINST MANY, YOU WILL ALMOST CERTAINLY BE OVERCOME IF YOU REMAIN IN ONE SPOT. THE AGGRESSORS ARE IRRATIONAL AND DEMENTED. THEIR SOLE URGE IS THEIR QUEST FOR HUMAN FLESH. SHERIFF CONAN W. MCCLELLAN, OF THE COUNTY DEPARTMENT OF PUBLIC PROTECTION, WAS INTERVIEWED MINUTES AFTER HE AND HIS VIGILANTE PATROL HAD VANQUISHED SEVERAL OF THE AGGRESSORS. WE BRING YOU NOW THE RESULTS OF THAT INTERVIEW..."

On the TV screen, the image of the commentator was replaced by newsreel footage, taken earlier that night. The footage showed dense woods, a dirt road, searchlights dancing among the trees, while men moved around peering into the darkness and shouting at one another. Sporadic distant gunfire could be heard over all this. Then the news camera showed footage of posted guards maintaining the periphery of a small clearing. Still, gunfire could be heard in the distance. Some of the men were smoking, others drinking coffee from paper containers or talking in small groups. The area was illuminated by a large bonfire. A closer shot revealed Sheriff McClellan, the central figure of the scene, shouting commands, supervising defensive measures, and at the same time trying to answer the reporter's questions as he paced around not straying too far—because of the cord and microphone hanging around his neck.

McClellan was a big man, gruff and used to commanding men and making them do what they were told in some semblance of order. He was dressed in civilian clothes, but carried a big rifle with scope and a belt of ammunition of heavy caliber.

At the moment, he had some of his men engaged in dragging bodies to the bonfire and throwing them on it to burn. The crackle of the bonfire, the shouts and bustle of activity, formed a constant background for McClellan's commentary as he did his best to answer what he was asked—while his primary concerns were his efforts in dealing with the aggressors and controlling his search party.

"Things ain't going too badly," McClellan said. "The men are taking it pretty well. We killed nineteen of those things today, right around this general area. These last three we found trying to claw their way into an abandoned mine shed—nobody was in there—but these things just pounding and clawing, trying to bust their way in. They must've thought there was people in there. We heard the racket and sneaked up on them and blasted them down."

"What's your opinion, then Sheriff? Can we defeat these things?"

"There ain't no problem—except just getting to them in time, before they kill off all the people that are trapped. But me and my men can handle them okay. We ain't lost nobody or suffered any casualties. All you gotta do is shoot for the brain. You can tell anybody out there—all you gotta do is draw a sharp bead and shoot for the brain—or beat 'em down and lop their heads off. They don't go anywhere once you chop their heads off. Then you gotta burn 'em."

"Then I'd have a decent chance, even if I was surrounded by two or three of them?"

"If you had yourself a club, or a good torch, you could hold 'em off or burn 'em to death. They catch fire like nothin'—go up like wax paper. But the best thing is to shoot for the brain. You don't want to get too close, unless you have to. Don't wait for us to rescue you, because if they get you too far outnumbered, you've had it. Their strength is in numbers. We're doin' our best—but we only got so many men and a whole lot of open country to comb."

"But you think you can bring the situation under control?"

"At least in our county. We got things in our favor now. It's only a question of time. We don't know for certain how many of them there are . . . but we know when we find 'em we're able to kill 'em. So it's a matter of time. They are weak—but there's pretty many of 'em. Don't wait for no rescue party. Arm yourself to the teeth, get together in a group, and try to make it to a rescue station—that's the best way. But if you're alone, you have to sit still and wait for help . . . and we'll try like hell to get you before they do."

"What are these things, Sheriff? In your opinion, what are they?"

"They're . . . they're dead. They're dead humans. That's all they are. Whatever brought 'em back and made 'em this way, I wish to God I knew—"

The television coverage had switched back to the live announcer, who resumed speaking in his matter-of-fact tone.

"... YOU HAVE HEARD SHERIFF CONAN W. MC-CLELLAN, OF THE COUNTY DEPARTMENT OF PUBLIC PROTECTION. THIS IS YOUR CIVIL DEFENSE

EMERGENCY NETWORK, WITH REPORTS EVERY HOUR ON THE HOUR, FOR THE DURATION OF THIS EMERGENCY. REMAIN IN YOUR HOMES. KEEP ALL DOORS AND WINDOWS LOCKED. DO NOT UNDER ANY CIRC—"

Ben reached over and clicked off the television.

Excited, Tom said, "Why'd you shut it off for?"

Ben shrugged. "The man said the reports only come on every hour. We heard all we need to know. We have to try and get out of here."

Helen agreed. "He said the rescue stations have doctors and medical supplies . . . if we could get there, they could help my daughter."

Harry laughed, scornfully. "How are we gonna bust out of here? We have a sick girl, a woman out of her head—and this place is crawling with those things."

"Willard is the nearest town," Tom said, ignoring Harry's objections. "They'd have a checkpoint there—about seventeen miles from here."

"You from here? You know the area?" Ben asked, excitedly.

"Sure," Tom replied, confidently. "Judy and I were going swimming up the road. We heard the news on her portable radio, and we came in here and found the lady dead upstairs. Not too long after, Harry and his wife and kid fought their way in here—I was scared, but I opened the basement door and let them in."

"Well, I think we ought to stick right here and wait for a rescue party," Harry said. "That fellow on the TV said if you're few against many, you don't have a chance—we can't hike seventeen miles cross-country through that army of things out there . . ."

"We don't have to tramp," Ben said. "My truck's right outside the door."

This stopped Harry. There was a long moment of silence while the fact of the truck sank into everybody's head.

"But I'm just about out of gas," Ben added. "There's a couple of gas pumps by the shed out back, but they're both locked up."

"The key ought to be around somewhere," Tom said. "There's a big key ring in the basement. I'll go look."

In his enthusiasm, now that escape seemed to be a possibility, he bolted for the cellar door and scampered down the stairs.

Ben turned to Harry. "Is there a fruit cellar down there?"

"Yeah. Why?"

"We're gonna need lots of jars. We can make Molotov cocktails... scare those things back... then fight our way to the pump and gas up the truck."

"We're gonna need kerosene, then," Harry said. "There's a jug of that in the basement, too."

Helen said, "Judy and I can help. We can rip up sheets and things." Then she added, in a hushed tone, "I don't think Barbara's going to be much help at all."

"How do you know her name?" Ben asked, startled.

"She was mumbling it in her sleep—something about her brother telling her over and over—Barbara, you're afraid. It must have happened just before he died."

There was a sudden clatter, and Tom came up out of the cellar. "Here's the key ring," he said. "The pump key is marked with a piece of tape. I talked with Judy. She's in favor of trying to escape."

"Good," Ben said. "Then nothing's holding us back. Anybody who's got any second thoughts better decide now. If that's the key for sure, we're in good shape—but we should take a crowbar anyway, in case the key doesn't work. The crowbar can double as a weapon for whoever goes with me. But I don't want to get all the way out there and find out we can't get the pump open."

"I'll go," Tom said. "You and me can fight our way to the pump. The women can stay in the cellar and take care of the kid. We should have a stretcher—Helen and Judy maybe can make one."

Ben turned to Harry and spoke sternly, emphasizing his words.

"Harry, you're gonna have to guard the upstairs. Once we unboard the front door, those things can get in here easily. But it has to stay unlocked, so me and Tom can get back in after we get back here with the truck. You've got to guard the door, and unlock it for us right away, 'cause we'll probably come flying on the run with a bunch of those things coming right behind us. We'll board the door up again as fast as we can once we're safe inside the house. If we don't get back, well, then you'll be able to see from upstairs, and you can barricade the door again and go to the basement—you and the rest can sit tight and hope for a rescue party."

Facing Ben, Harry said, "I want the gun, then. It's the best thing for me to use. You're not going to have time to stop and aim—"

Ben cut him off, in no uncertain terms.

"I'm keeping this gun. Nobody else lays a hand on it. I found it, and it's mine."

Harry said, "How do we know you and Tom won't just get the truck gassed up and cut out?"

Ben glowered, trying to control his anger. "That's the chance you have to take," he said evenly and forcefully. "If we cut out, you'll have your goddamn basement—like you've been crying about all along."

"We're going to die here," Helen said, pleadingly, "if we don't all work together."

Ben looked at her, sizing her up. He had pretty much decided she was not a coward, like her husband. He'd almost rather have her guarding the front door—but she was not nearly as strong as Harry, provided he did not chicken out.

Ben addressed all of them, in commanding tones.

"Let's get busy. More of those things are coming to surround us all the time. And we've got a lot to do if we're gonna bust out of here. If everything goes right, two or three hours from now we'll be taking a hot shower in the Willard Hotel."

Nobody laughed.

They separated, each to begin his or her assigned task.

Ben turned the radio back on. It began repeating its recorded message. The time was approximately 11:30. One half-hour to go until midnight, when there would be another regular broadcast.

It would come in the middle of their escape preparations. They could take time out to watch it on the television, in case it contained current information that might prove helpful.

In the meantime, there was nothing to do . . . but to work hard . . . and to hope.

Chapter 7

Helen and Harry Cooper came down into the basement and found Judy watching over the sick girl, Karen, who now seemed a little delirious. She tossed and turned, and moaned softly now and then, as she lay on the makeshift worktable.

"Has she asked for me?" Helen asked, intently. "Has she spoken at all?"

Harry reached down and covered his daughter, where she had shaken off the coat that was covering her, in her delirium.

"She's been moaning and crying out constantly," Judy said, her face showing her worry and concern for the child.

"Poor baby!" Helen sighed, and she touched her hand to Karen's forehead and felt the increase of fever.

"Get another damp cloth," Harry said. "I'm going to start making a stretcher. Judy, I'll give you the box of fruit jars over there, and you take them up to Tom. He'll have to come down here for the kerosene. We're going to make Molotov cocktails."

The idea of making something like that seemed weird to Judy, like something she had seen but only vaguely understood, from the movies. She knew a Molotov cocktail was something that caught fire when you threw it at a tank, but she had no idea how to make one. But she stood waiting patiently while Harry dug out the old, dusty box of fruit jars and loaded it into her arms. It wasn't heavy, but she was too loaded down to carry anything else.

"You'll have to send Tom back down for the kerosene," Harry repeated. "Helen and I will take care of Karen and start making the stretcher. Tell Tom to bring us some old sheets or blankets."

Harry watched after her, as she climbed the stairs out of the cellar, as though she would be likely not to do it right if he didn't watch her. "We'll be damned lucky if we make it," he said, turning to Helen. "It would be tough enough for half a dozen men to beat their way through those things."

Helen looked up from where she had been applying her dampened cloth to Karen's forehead. She didn't say anything to combat Harry's pessimism; she merely trembled. As her eyes looked into the fever-tossed, agonized face of her young daughter, she caught her breath and almost did not dare to hope that they would make it.

"Lord help us," she mumbled, when her breath came to her again.

Over by the workbench, Harry had begun pounding on something, in his effort to fashion a crude stretcher.

Chapter 8

Ben had returned to the vacant room, which contained the mutilated corpse of the old lady who had once lived there. The vacant room was the one that looked out onto the front lawn, and Harry would have to station himself there to toss Molotov cocktails from the window.

Ben held his breath and tried not to look at the corpse, but he knew he had to get it out of the room. Seeing a thing like that was the very thing which was likely to spook Harry and bring his cowardice trembling to the surface—and then he would panic and run, and fail to do the job that was expected of him.

The entire room smelled of the rotting corpse, which had been closed in there for a couple of hours. Ben had to step into the hall for a while, to allow the room to air out. He went into the bathroom and lifted the window an inch or two, and sucked cold night air into his nostrils—but the scent of the dead things outside came to him faintly, mingled with the normal odors of dampness and freshly cut grass and plowed fields. The man closed the bathroom window and returned to the room which he hated to enter.

He began dragging the corpse out into the hallway and toward the child's room across the hall. On its blood-crusted carpet, it slid along fairly easily on the bare floor, but when it reached the rug in the child's room, it balked and was harder to drag. Ben grunted, gagged with the stench of a lungful of the dead woman's odor, and with a desperate heave got it into the room, near the bunk bed, stepped over it quickly to get out of there, and slammed the door.

Again, he went to the bathroom and opened the window enough to suck in "fresh" air.

When he returned to the vacant room, it still smelled bad, but not as bad as before. He went to the window, taking pains to keep his body pressed close against the wall, where he could not be seen very easily. With his hand, he rubbed a clean spot on the dirty, uncurtained window.

There were now at least thirty of the things standing down there on the front lawn. And, in the fields beyond, several more could be seen, making their way toward the house.

CHAPTER 9

Barbara was sitting up, by the fire. She had a morose, almost vacant, expression on her face, as though she no longer cared whether she lived or died.

In the corner of the room that had once been the dining area, Tom and Judy were making Molotov cocktails. Judy was using a pair of scissors to cut up an old bedsheet into strips, while Tom was filling the fruit jars with kerosene from a can. Then, together, they began soaking the cloth strips in kerosene in the bottom of a dish and forcing these makeshift fuses through holes which Tom had cut in the caps of the jars.

They worked silently for a long time, but when Judy looked over at Barbara, sitting so inert and morbid on the sofa, with the fire flickering in her face, she felt a need to make conversation—to relieve the silence.

"Tom . . . do you think we're doing the right thing?" she asked suddenly, looking up from her task with the fuses. She stared at her hands, with the odor of kerosene coming off them.

Tom looked at her and smiled, tensely but reassuringly. "Sure, honey. I don't think we have a chance if we stay here. There are more and more of those things all the time. The television broadcast advised anyone who was in a situation like ours to try to escape."

"But—what about the rescue parties?"

"We can't take a chance on waiting. Nobody might ever come to help us. Think how many people must be trapped, like we are."

Judy fell silent as she returned to her task with the fuses.

"I think we're going to make it," Tom said. "We're not all that far from the gas pumps. And Ben said he beat down three of those things before. And now we have the gun."

He looked at her intently, noticing the worried look on her face, which he had never before seen in the short time they had been going together.

"But . . . why do you have to be the one to go out there?" she said finally.

"Honey, you're talking like Harry Cooper now. Somebody has to go. We can't just sit here and wait for those things to kill us. Besides, we're gonna be all right—you wait and see. We're gonna make it."

She leaned forward and put her arms around him, awkwardly, trying to touch him with her kerosened hands.

About to kiss, they were startled by the loud sound of Harry's footsteps, coming up out of the basement. A tense look on his face, he entered the room and said angrily, "What's the matter? Doesn't anybody keep their head around here? It's almost time for another broadcast."

"Five more minutes," Tom said, looking at his wristwatch.

"Well, we've got to get the damned thing warmed up," Harry said, and he stepped over to the television and turned it on just as Ben came down from the upstairs.

"What's going on?" Ben said.

"Another broadcast," Tom answered, and to show Ben he had not been loafing he continued working with the fuses, dipping them and forcing them into the bottles.

Ben moved over to Barbara and looked at her, shaking his head sadly.

"Goddamn this television," Harry said. "It takes half a century to warm up. We could all die waiting for it."

He nervously struck a match and lit a cigarette, while the picture tube began to glow and the sound came on.

"We've got to get that girl down into the basement," Harry added, with a glance in Barbara's direction. "She's no good to herself or anyone else up here."

Nobody made a reply to Harry's comment, and they all fell silent as the news broadcast came on. It was a different commentator, but the newsroom was the same, with its multitude of clocks on the wall showing what time it was in various parts of the nation, and its background of ticker-tape sounds and blurred human voices.

"GOOD EVENING, LADIES AND GENTLEMEN. IT IS NOW MIDNIGHT, EASTERN TIME. THIS IS YOUR CIVIL DEFENSE NETWORK, WITH REPORTS EVERY HOUR ON THE HOUR FOR THE DURATION OF THIS... EMERGENCY. STAY TUNED TO THIS WAVELENGTH FOR SURVIVAL INFORMATION.

"LADIES AND GENTLEMEN... INCREDIBLE AS IT MAY SEEM... THE LATEST REPORT FROM THE PRESIDENT'S RESEARCH TEAM AT WALTER READE HOSPITAL CONFIRMS WHAT MANY OF US HAVE ACCEPTED AS FACT WITHOUT BOTHERING TO WAIT FOR OFFICIAL CONFIRMATION. THE ARMY OF AGGRESSORS WHICH HAS BESIEGED MANY OF THE EASTERN AND MIDWESTERN SECTIONS OF OUR COUNTRY IS MADE UP OF DEAD HUMAN BEINGS."

Judy shuddered as the announcer paused, allowing time for his statement to sink in. The expression on his face showed that he hardly believed it himself.

"I didn't need him to tell me that," Ben said.

"Quiet!" Harry yelled.

"THE RECENTLY DEAD HAVE BEEN RETURNING TO LIFE AND FEASTING ON HUMAN FLESH. DEAD

PEOPLE FROM MORGUES, HOSPITALS, FUNERAL PARLORS... AS WELL AS MANY OF THOSE KILLED DURING OR AS A RESULT OF THE CHAOS CREATED DURING THIS EMERGENCY... HAVE BEEN RETURNED TO LIFE IN A DEPRAVED, INCOMPLETE FORM... WITH AN URGE TO KILL OTHER HUMANS AND DEVOUR THEIR FLESH.

"EXPLANATIONS FOR THE CAUSES OF THIS INCREDIBLE PHENOMENON HAVE NOT BEEN FORTHCOMING FROM THE WHITE HOUSE OR FROM POSITIONS OF AUTHORITY, BUT SPECULATION CENTERS ON THE RECENT VENUS PROBE, WHICH WAS UNSUCCESSFUL. THAT ROCKET SHIP, YOU REMEMBER, STARTED FOR VENUS MORE THAN A WEEK AGO—BUT NEVER GOT THERE. INSTEAD, IT RETURNED TO EARTH, CARRYING A MYSTERIOUS HIGH-LEVEL RADIATION WITH IT. COULD THAT RADIATION HAVE BEEN RESPONSIBLE FOR THE WHOLESALE MURDER WE ARE NOW WITNESSING? SPECULATION ON THE ANSWER TO THAT QUESTION HAS RUN RAMPANT HERE IN WASHINGTON AND ELSEWHERE, WHILE THE WHITE HOUSE HAS MAINTAINED A CURTAIN OF SILENCE AND HAS ATTEMPTED TO DEAL WITH THIS EMERGENCY BY PHYSICAL MEANS—THAT IS, BY ORGANIZING RESISTANCE AND SEARCH AND DESTROY MISSIONS AGAINST THE... AGGRESSORS. MEETINGS AT THE PENTAGON AND THE WHITE HOUSE HAVE REMAINED CLOSED TO REPORTERS, AND MEMBERS OF THE MILITARY AND CIVILIAN ADVISORS HAVE REFUSED TO CONDUCT INTERVIEWS OR TO ANSWER QUESTIONS THRUST AT THEM BY REPORTERS, ON THE WAY TO OR FROM SUCH MEETINGS.

"HOWEVER, THE LATEST OFFICIAL COMMUNIQUÉ FROM THE PENTAGON HAS CONFIRMED THAT THE AGGRESSORS ARE DEAD. THEY ARE NOT INVADERS

FROM ANOTHER PLANET. THEY ARE THE RECENTLY DEAD FROM RIGHT HERE ON EARTH. NOT ALL OF THE RECENTLY DEAD HAVE RETURNED TO LIFE—BUT IN CERTAIN AREAS OF THE COUNTRY, THE EAST AND MIDWEST IN PARTICULAR, THE PHENOMENON IS MORE WIDESPREAD THAN ELSEWHERE. WHY THE MIDWEST SHOULD BE AN AREA SO GREATLY AFFLICTED IS NOT EASILY EXPLAINED, EVEN BY THE MOST CALCULATED SPECULATION. THE VENUS PROBE, YOU REMEMBER, CRASHED IN THE ATLANTIC OCEAN, JUST OFF THE EASTERN SEABOARD.

"PERHAPS WE SHALL NEVER KNOW THE EXACT REASONS FOR THE TERRIBLE PHENOMENON WE ARE NOW WITNESSING.

"THERE IS SOME HOPE, HOWEVER, THAT THE MENACE WILL BE BROUGHT UNDER CONTROL... PERHAPS IN A MATTER OF SEVERAL DAYS OR WEEKS. THE... AGGRESSORS... CAN BE KILLED BY GUNSHOT OR A HEAVY BLOW TO THE HEAD. THEY ARE AFRAID OF FIRE, AND THEY BURN EASILY. THEY HAVE ALL THE CHARACTERISTICS OF DEAD PEOPLE... EXCEPT THEY ARE NOT DEAD—FOR REASONS WE DO NOT AS YET UNDERSTAND, THEIR BRAINS HAVE BEEN ACTIVATED AND THEY ARE CANNIBALS.

"IN ADDITION, ANYONE WHO DIES FROM A WOUND INFLICTED BY THE FLESH-EATERS MAY HIMSELF COME BACK TO LIFE IN THE SAME FORM AS THE AGGRESSORS THEMSELVES. THE DISEASE THAT THESE THINGS CARRY IS COMMUNICABLE THROUGH OPEN FLESH WOUNDS OR SCRATCHES, AND TAKES EFFECT MINUTES AFTER THE APPARENT DEATH OF THE WOUNDED PERSON. ANYONE WHO DIES DURING THIS EMERGENCY SHOULD BE IMMEDIATELY DECAPITATED OR CREMATED. SUR-

VIVORS WILL FIND THESE MEASURES DIFFICULT TO UNDERTAKE, BUT THEY MUST BE UNDERTAKEN ANYWAY, OR ELSE THE AUTHORITIES MUST BE ALERTED TO UNDERTAKE IT FOR YOU. THOSE WHO DIE DURING THIS EMERGENCY ARE NOT CORPSES IN THE USUAL SENSE, THEY ARE DEAD FLESH—BUT HIGHLY DANGEROUS AND A THREAT TO ALL LIFE ON OUR PLANET. I REPEAT, THEY MUST BE BURNED OR DECAPITATED..."

A shudder went through Harry, and all the eyes in the room turned on him.

"How did your kid get hurt?" Ben asked.

"One of those things grabbed her, while we were all trying to run. I'm not sure—but I think she was bitten on the arm."

They all stared at Harry, feeling sorry for him, but realizing at the same time the threat Karen would be to them, if she died.

"You or Helen had better stay with her at all times," Ben warned. "If she doesn't pull through... well..."

His voice trailed off.

Harry covered his face with his hands, as he tried to accept the thought of what he would have to do. Knowing his daughter might die had been bad enough but now—

Another shudder went through him.

The people in the living room had their eyes glued to the tube and were avoiding looking in Harry's direction.

"You'll have to tell Helen what to expect," Ben said. "Otherwise, she won't know how to deal with it if it happens."

Ben thought of his own children, and trembled with anguish and homesickness for them. Then he forced his attention back to the television, in case he might learn something that would be of value in trying to escape.

But the tube faded to a glow.

The broadcast was over.

Clattering his chair, Tom got to his feet. "We'd better get started," he said. "There's nothing more we can do here."

Ben slung his gun over his shoulder, as he bent to pick up a claw hammer and crowbar. Facing Harry, he said, "You've got to station yourself in the empty room upstairs. All women will stay in the cellar. Soon as Tom and I have the front door unboarded, you start tossing the Molotov cocktails. Make sure they catch fire good— throw every one of them—but don't hit the truck. If you can catch a couple of those things on fire, so much the better. When we hear your footsteps on the stairs, me and Tom'll be gone. It'll be up to you Harry—you've got to guard the front door. Got yourself a good length of pipe?"

"I have a pitchfork."

"Good . . . okay."

While Ben delivered his instructions, Tom knelt near the fire and soaked a table-leg in kerosene so it would make a good torch.

With a little coaxing, Judy got Barbara to her feet and ushered her down into the basement. But Tom turned, as he had heard only one pair of feet descending the stairs. Judy stood looking at him from behind the half-opened cellar door—an anguished look on her face as Harry left the room with his box of Molotov cocktails and Tom began to help Ben unboard the front door.

Judy worried and watched in silence, while the man and the boy engaged in the painstaking work of very quietly undoing the barricade, so as not to give alarm to the lurking things outside. With crowbar and claw hammer, slowly and carefully, both Tom and Ben worked on each piece of lumber. Each nail-creak was a menace. They were alert to the constant danger—until the barricade was finally undone.

Tom lit the torch and handed it to Ben, and they posted themselves by the door, waiting for the Molotov shower to begin.

Ben shifted the curtain and peered outside, sizing up the situation they were about to plunge themselves into. On the lawn, under the trees, many shadowy figures were lurking, silent and threatening in the darkness; several of the dead things were standing near the truck—it was going to be a hard fight for Tom and Ben to get into it. And across the field, along the route that the truck would have to take to the gas pumps, many more of the flesh-eaters were watching and waiting.

If anything went wrong, they would never get back to the house alive.

Judy still had not gone down into the cellar. Her eyes were fastened on Tom, as if she wanted to continue seeing him until the last possible moment—because once he was gone out into the night she might never see him again.

Suddenly—a cry from upstairs. A window flew open, and the first fiery blaze lit the yard.

Ben flung the front door open, and in the glow of the blazing kerosene fire he watched as the creatures moaned with their hideous rasping sounds and began clutching at themselves dumbly and backing slowly away. More cocktails followed, crashing in the yard with a splintering sound as the flames leaped up and illuminated the old truck and the eerie dead things that had been stationed around it.

Several of the things caught fire and walked and staggered with the flames—their dead flesh popping and crackling and burning with a terrible stench—until they were consumed by the fire and brought down by it, not killed but immobilized, still moving and making rasping sounds until there was not sufficient body left to continue to move any longer . . .

Still, the bombs showered from upstairs. The field beyond the house was now lit up dimly, the shadows of trees and bushes moving eerily and changing complexion as each new puddle of fire took hold and the flames rose and fell.

Ben and Tom stood on the porch, watching the dead things burning and backing away, while they kept their weapons ready to use on any of the beings who might attack before they were to make their break for the truck.

"That's all Ben—run for it!"

Harry shouted from upstairs, slamming the door to the vacant room and scurrying for the stairs.

His voice echoed, as Tom and Ben burst into the yard, surrounded by puddles of flame and threatened by the dead ghouls, some of which were starting to move forward, their fear of fire not as strong as their urge for human flesh.

Tom clubbed at one of the attackers with the crowbar and it went down, but it was still struggling on the ground. Ben stabbed at it with the torch, and it caught fire and burst into a blaze as it began to die, clutching at itself.

Harry had gotten to the front door—too late to stop Judy from running out onto the lawn. "I'm going with them!" she screamed, and Harry clutched at her, but she ran right by him and stopped, caught short, when he slammed the front door.

Two of the ghouls were coming for her; she could not get back inside, and her way to the truck was blocked.

She screamed, and Ben turned and saw her while Tom leaped into the driver's seat of the truck. One of the things was clutching at him, and he had to drive it back by kicking it hard in the chest.

Ben wheeled and clubbed at the two ghouls in front of Judy. The shock of the rifle thudded against their dead skulls and brought them to the earth, each with a sickening crunch and a splintering of bone that was already dead.

Ben grabbed the frightened girl and pushed her into the truck, then leaped into the bed of it as Tom's eyes fell on Judy and the truck lurched out. It careened and skidded in a U-turn for the old shed and the gas pumps across the field. Several ghouls, clawing and pounding at the humans inside, fell away from the truck as it moved—and Ben set still another one on fire with his torch and beat at it as it continued to try to hang on even while it was burning—until it was shaken loose finally and fell with its head under the tire of the truck.

Temporarily in the clear, Tom raced the truck across the field, while many of the ghouls followed after, staggering slowly but in relentless pursuit of their objective. Ben aimed and fired several shots cocking and firing in rapid succession—and wasting ammunition, actually—as most of his shots missed as the truck jounced over the ruts in the grassy field, but one creature went down, with half its skull blown completely away.

The others continued to follow after the old truck, as it screeched to a halt in front of the gas pumps and the shed, and Tom and Ben leaped out. Still more attackers were approaching, several parties of them now making their way across the field. Tom fumbled with the key to the locked pumps. Ben shoved him back, hurriedly aimed the gun and fired, blowing the lock to pieces. Gas spurted all over the place, as Ben handed the torch to Tom so he would have some means of protecting himself—he had left his crowbar in the truck.

Her eyes wide with fear, Judy stared through the windshield, first at Tom, then out into the field, as the creatures continued to advance. Several of them were less than thirty yards away.

Gas still spurting, Tom crammed the nozzle into the mouth of the gas tank and his torch fell from his hands onto the gasoline-soaked ground. Tongues of flame leaped up—and set fire to the truck.

The rear fender was burning. Ben saw it out of the corner of his eye as he crouched and leveled off with his weapon and fired. An approaching attacker went down but got back up again, a gaping hole in its chest, just below the neck.

In force of numbers, the attackers continued to advance.

Tom stared at the truck as the flames began to lick and spread. Ben stared, too, momentarily—he did not know what to do. Then he wheeled and yelled, as Tom leaped into the flaming truck and it lurched and skidded across the field, plowing down some of the attackers in its way. Tom wanted to get the truck away from the gas pumps, to prevent them from exploding. Ben yelled again, but to no avail, as the flaming truck sped away, driven by the panicked Tom—Judy scared speechless beside him in the front seat.

Several of the things were upon Ben. He thrashed and pounded at them with the torch and gun. Figuring that Tom was lost, he knew he had to try and fight his own way back to the house.

Ben succeeded in setting fire to two of the ghouls that were attacking him and beating a third one to the ground.

He ran, swinging the torch and gun, spinning in all directions so as not to be brought down from behind. The stench of the ghouls alone was almost overpowering as mobs of them threatened to close in and tear him apart.

From inside the house, Harry had been able to see only pieces of the action, although he kept darting back and forth from door to window, squinting through the barricades, trying to make sure of what was going on outside. From his point of view the escape attempt seemed to have met with total doom—and if so, he wanted to lock the front door and run into the basement and barricade it.

Harry saw the truck catch fire—and saw Tom drive it away. As for Ben, he appeared to be overwhelmed. Harry ran to another window.

The truck, almost completely in flames, was speeding away from the house, toward a small rise. Eerily, it was lighting up its own path as it lurched and bounced along in the otherwise pitch-black field. Suddenly it screeched to a halt. Harry could see a figure, that of Tom, crawling out of the driver's side and trying to help Judy get out, too. Then—an overpowering blast. The truck exploded violently, the noise and flames shattering the night.

In the midst of his struggles with the ghouls, Ben looked up and shuddered as he realized what had happened to Judy and Tom. The flames from the exploded truck helped him to see his way clear to fight a little nearer to the house. With powerful, desperate blows from his torch and gun, Ben continued to beat back his attackers in a life-or-death attempt to gain safety.

Several ghouls were at the front door, trying to beat their way into the house. From inside, Harry was in complete terror. Finally, heedless of anybody's plight but his own, he panicked and bolted for the cellar.

But Ben had slugged his way through the attackers on the porch—and now he was pounding for admission at the front door. Spinning, with a powerful lunge he kicked the last attacker off the porch; in the rebound he ploughed his shoulder against the door; it crashed open and Ben burst through in time to catch Harry at the cellar door.

But there was no time to redress Harry. Ben turned frantically to re-boarding the door as his eyes met Harry's for an instant and they both fell to work—as if Harry thought he could maintain some vestige of respect in Ben's eyes by pitching in and helping now.

They managed to get the door boarded up. The house was temporarily safe.

They turned and looked at each other, Harry shaking with fear, sweat streaming from his face. Both men knew what was coming—and Ben's fist crashed against Harry's face even as he was attempting to back away.

Harry was driven back, one punch after another, until Ben cornered him and slammed him against the wall and held him there, staring into his face. Ben spat his words out, each word punctuated by an additional slam of Harry against the wall.

"You ... rotten ... goddamn ... next ... time ... you do something ... like that ... I'll drag you outside and feed ... you ... to those things!"

Ben slammed him one final time, and he slid down the wall and crumpled on the floor, his face bruised and his nose streaming with blood.

Ben moved to the cellar door.

"Come on up! It's us ... It's all over ... Tom and Judy are dead!"

He pivoted, hurled himself across the room to a window, and saw the ghouls moving closer to the house. Despite his exhaustion, he shuddered.

What on earth were they going to do now?

Chapter 10

By midnight, Sheriff McClellan and his men had established the camp where they intended to bed down for the night. They had kept on the march until the sun sank low enough to make it impossible to go any farther, then on McClellan's command they had pitched camp in an open field where any approaching aggressors would be easy to spot because of the absence of concealing foliage; to make doubly sure the place was secure from attack, they had posted guards and established a periphery of defense.

Luckily, the night was warm and without any threat of rain. Most of the men had blankets and sleeping bags but there were very few tents. The posse had been organized in too big a hurry, and a lot of its members were inexperienced and did not have the proper gear for living in the woods; in addition to the normally difficult problems of feeding and supplying a posse of forty or fifty men, there had been a myriad of pesky complaints common to novices—like poison ivy and blistered feet.

Through it all, McClellan had alternately bullied and pampered the men, to keep them on the move in a disciplined fashion, combing the rural areas in search of those who might require aid or rescue—until nightfall made it unwise to try to proceed any further. Then, reluctantly, the gruff sheriff had given the order to pitch camp and had supervised the establishment of it and the maintenance of proper defenses.

The men were tired. But the warmth of the campfires and smell of hot coffee went a long way toward reviving their flagging spirits; and, not too long after midnight a van arrived loaded down with box lunches for all the men so they would not have to bed down hungry. Candles and Coleman lanterns burned in various parts of the camp, giving it from a distance a rustic but cheerful look, and here and there a card game got started despite the fact that they all knew they'd have to break camp and be on the move without any breakfast, come dawn.

McClellan sat by himself just outside his tent, listening to the murmur of surrounding voices and the occasional rattle of a fork or spoon or a heavier piece of equipment. His maps were spread out on a field table in front of him, lighted by an overhanging lantern with a buzzing circle of gnats and other insects that intermittently annoyed McClellan by flying into his face. He was impatient to finish with the maps so he could extinguish the lantern and turn in for the night.

With his red pencil, he made a mark on the spot he knew to be his position—fifteen miles north of a little town called Willard. Still farther north, for a stretch of several miles, there were scattered farmhouses and a tiny village or two where the inhabitants were relatively isolated and presumed to be in dire need of help, although the status of any of the families in the area still to be combed by McClellan's posse was largely a matter of speculation, because of the communications breakdown that had occurred in the early stages of the emergency.

The county had been divided into sectors, each sector to be patrolled by a combination of posse volunteers and National Guard troops. The objectives were to reestablish communications in areas where lines were down or power stations were out of commission; to bring safety and law and order to villages and larger communities, where order was threatened not only by marauding ghouls but by looters and rapists taking advantage of the chaos created by the emergency; and to send rescue parties out into rural or remote areas, where people could be trapped in their homes with no way of defending themselves adequately or calling for help.

McClellan's sector happened to be a particularly dangerous one. In addition to the normal number of recently dead from hospitals, morgues and funeral homes, a bus full of people—the driver frightened by several of the dead things suddenly appearing in front of him as he rounded a curve—had crashed through a guard rail and over an embankment, killing everyone on board, presumably, but when McClellan's posse found the bus there were only a few ghouls wandering around aimlessly, and these were gunned down and burned. One of them, with several shattered rib bones protruding through the front of its chest, was wearing a bus driver's uniform; and from that McClellan was pretty certain of what had happened to the other people. Long before the offficial announcement was made public, McClellan and his men, working hard out in the endangered areas, knew that the aggressors were dead humans and that anyone who died was likely to become an aggressor. Although many of the men carried knives and machetes to protect themselves against wounds and contamination, their procedure was to avoid tangling with the flesh-eaters at close range, by gunning them down at a distance; then, by making use of meat-hooks, they would drag the dead things to a pile, soak them with gasoline, and set fire to them. Anyone who had touched a meat-hook, or anything suspected of having been in contact with a ghoul, would wash his hands with plenty of soap and water and afterward in a solution of alcohol. It was not known whether or not these measures would be totally effective, but they had seemed to be so far—and nobody could think of what else to do, under the circumstances.

As McClellan had stated earlier in his news interview, his posse had suffered no losses and no casualties in the eight hours or so that it had been in the field.

By splitting up into squads at times, they had managed to cover quite a number of isolated farmhouses during the hard day's trek, and had rescued some and had found some dead—

with the flesh picked from their bodies. They had also gunned down quite a few, when it could be seen that they were no longer dead—or human.

Now, with a day's experience behind him, the sheriff had the means to gauge and evaluate the task that lay before him; and looking on the map at the territory that remained to be combed, he figured he could do it in three or four more days, by pushing the men hard. He hated to push men—but he was good at it, and there were situations, like this one, where it was absolutely necessary; a lot of lives might depend on just how quickly the posse was able to get to them.

As McClellan slapped at a gnat that had lighted on his forehead, a heavy shadow fell across his map table and he looked up to see his deputy, George Henderson.

George was a strong, wiry man of medium height, wearing hunting clothes that looked well-worn and fitted his body the way that clothes will do when they are used to the body that is wearing them. He unslung his rifle and scratched the stubble of beard on his chin.

"You're standing in my light," McClellan said gruffly, his head tilted downward as though to continue scrutinizing his map.

George gave a snort, which was intended to pass as a laugh, and stepped aside, disappointed that he could not think of a wisecrack to hurl back at McClellan. Instead, he said, "I checked the guards. Five of the bastards were asleep."

"You're kidding," McClellan said, shoving himself away from his map table as though he would stomp out and crucify the five men.

"Yep," George said.

He meant, yep, he was kidding. He chuckled, and this time McClellan was the one who merely snorted.

"All the guards are posted," George said. "I made them take black coffee to stay awake."

"If any of those things get into this camp with these men in sleeping bags—"

"A lot of them are keeping pistols in their sleeping bags with them. And the ones that don't have pistols are keeping their rifles or machetes close by."

"We ought to keep the fires going," McClellan said. "Tell the next change of guards to keep feeding the fires all night."

"Okay," George said. "But I already thought of it. I was going to tell them anyway."

McClellan snorted, as though George couldn't possibly think of such a concept on his own.

"You're just pissed off because you didn't think of it first," George said, and he pulled up a field chair and sat down a few feet from the table. "Am I sitting in your light?" he asked, with a tone of mock sarcasm.

"Why don't you go get yourself a cup of coffee?" was McClellan's only reply—as though he was suggesting it merely to get rid of George.

"Did you get any?" George asked.

"Nope. I don't want it to keep me awake."

"You're gonna be snoozing like a big panda bear, while these men are standing watch and I'm out half the night checking the guards."

"If you were capable of the brain work, I'd hand it over to you," McClellan said, kidding. "Then you'd be the one to sleep. As it is, I've got to keep my mind fresh so this organization doesn't fall to pieces."

"Hah! That's a good one!" George exclaimed. "If it wasn't for me doin' the shit-work, these men would all be playin' cards or shootin' marbles—"

"I want everybody out of their sacks at four-thirty," McClellan broke in, in a serious tone.

"What?"

"Four-thirty. We've got to break camp and be on the move soon as we can see to navigate. Any time we spend screwin' around could mean somebody else dead."

"How much you figure on doin' tomorrow?"

"I got ten farmhouses I'd like to cover before noon. You can take a look at the map and see which ones. If we get that far, we'll break for lunch. We can radio ahead and let them know where we're gonna be."

George bent over the map and peered at it. The farmhouses that the sheriff intended to cover, marked in red, were back off a road shown on the map as a two-lane blacktop. The field where the posse was presently camped lay about two or three miles south of the blacktop road, and they had been marching in its direction all the previous day, advancing generally toward it with digressions as squads of men branched out in flanking movements to cover scattered dwellings before returning to the main body of the posse.

McClellan lit a cigarette and dragged on it, while George scrutinized their previous route and sized up the one that lay ahead.

The last house in their anticipated line of march was the old Miller farm, where Mrs. Miller—if she was still alive—lived with her grandson, Jimmy, a boy eleven years old.

"We ought to send out a separate patrol to get to this place," George said, pointing to the red X that marked the Miller farm on McClellan's map. "I know Mrs. Miller. She'd be pretty helpless. She and her grandson are all alone out there."

"We should be there before noon," McClellan said. "If they ain't dead already, they should be all right."

"I'm going to get me some coffee," George said. "Then I'm gonna rustle the second round of guards out of their sacks."

Chapter 11

Surprisingly, considering the violence of the explosion, the truck stopped burning rather quickly. It had not had much gasoline in it, and when that was gone there was very little about the truck that was combustible. Just the seats and the upholstery. And the human bodies inside.

The metal, with its paint charred and blistered, cooled rapidly in the night air.

And the ghouls came forward, slowly at first, and clustered around the truck. The smell of burning flesh drew them closer. But the hot metal at first prevented them from attaining what enticed them and was so near to their grasp.

When the metal was cold as death and smoke no longer curled from the ruins of the truck, the flesh-eaters moved in like vultures.

Tom and Judy could not feel their limbs being torn from their dead bodies. They could not hear bones and cartilage being twisted and broken and separated at the joints. They could not cry out when the ravenous ghouls ripped out their hearts and lungs and kidneys and intestines.

The ghouls fought among themselves, clawed and struggled with each other for possession of the once living organs; then, when possession was asserted, they went off—each to hover alone in near-privacy, except for other hungry ghouls looking on—to devour whatever organ or piece of a human body the lucky ones had managed to claim. They were like dogs, dragging their bones off to a corner to chew and gnaw, while other dogs looked on.

Several of the ghouls, in search of a comfortable place to eat where they would not have to defend their meals from one another, found refuge in the darkened front lawn of the old farmhouse, under the big silent trees.

There they waited patiently and watched the house—and ate, while the sound of teeth biting and ripping into dead human flesh and bone filled the night air. And, constantly, there was the rasp of crickets and the rasp of the heavy breathing of dead lungs mingling with the other night sounds.

CHAPTER 12

Inside the house, the mood was one of hopelessness and despair. Barbara was once again sitting on the sofa, her vacant eyes staring into space. Harry was sulking in a corner, his head slung back in a rocking chair that creaked every time he moved, which was not very often; his face was swollen; he was holding an ice-pack against his eye. His other eye, like a wandering sentinel, followed Ben who was pacing about the room; when Ben's pacing took him to the kitchen, or to some area out of Harry's sight, the good eye nervously relaxed a little. Ben's movements made virtually the only sound in the room, other than the occasional creaking of Harry's rocking chair.

Ben was checking the defenses, by force of habit rather than hope, while his rifle remained slung on his back. With the failure of the escape attempt, he had allowed himself to become almost totally dejected; he felt as powerless as the others who were imprisoned in the house with him. He could not think of what to try next in order to escape, yet he knew that in time they would all be doomed if they stayed put. Harry continued to watch with his good eye, while Ben paced from door to kitchen to window; he started to go upstairs, stopped, checked himself, went to the door again.

Suddenly, there was a noise on the cellar stairs and Helen entered the living room. "It's ten minutes to three," she said, to no one in particular. "There'll be another broadcast in ten more minutes."

Nobody said anything.

"Maybe the situation has improved somehow," Helen said, without feeling much of a basis for it.

"You or Harry had better get downstairs and maintain a watch over your kid," Ben said.

"In a little while," Helen said, after a long pause. "I want to watch the broadcast first."

Ben looked at her, as though to give her an argument, but he held his tongue; he was too tired and depressed to haggle with anybody. He only hoped the little girl didn't die while they were all watching the television.

Turning his back on the people in the room, he peeled back the curtain and peered through the window of the barricaded front door. Suddenly his eyes widened with fear and revulsion, but he continued to watch for a long time. There were many ghouls lurking in the shadows of the trees. Some of the things were out in the open, much nearer the house than they had dared come before. The remains of the charred bodies of several ghouls felled during the escape attempt were dimly apparent on various parts of the lawn; for some as yet unaccountable reason, the flesh-eaters never bothered to devour one of their own; they preferred fresh human meat.

And some of the ghouls had what they wanted, for Ben's eyes were fastened on a truly grisly scene; at the edge of the lawn, in the moonlight, several ghouls were devouring what had once been Tom . . . and Judy. They were ripping and tearing into pieces of human bodies . . . ghoulish teeth . . . biting into human arms and hands and fingers . . . sucking and chewing on human hearts and lungs. Ben stared . . . fascinated . . . and repulsed . . .

With a convulsive movement, his fingers released the curtain as he spun around, badly shaken, and faced the others, beads of perspiration on his forehead.

"Don't . . . don't . . . none of you look out there," Ben said, holding his stomach to keep from gagging. "You won't like what you see."

Harry's good eye fastened on Ben and watched him, satisfied and contemptuous to see the big man weaken. Ben moved for the television and clicked it on.

Barbara's scream pierced the room. Ben jumped back from the television. She was on her feet, screaming uncontrollably.

"We'll never get out of here... None of us! We'll never get out of here alive Johneeee! Johneee!... Oh! Oh... GOD... None of us... None of us... Help... Oh God... God...!"

Before anyone could move to her, she choked up as suddenly as she had begun and slumped, sobbing violently, to the couch, her face buried in her hands. Helen tried to soothe her, but great sobs came wracking from deep within. As she grew gradually quiet, the sobs diminished and stopped, but she remained slumped on the couch, her face covered with her hands. Helen pulled the overcoat over her, but the action seemed so futile—Barbara made no reaction whatsoever.

Ben allowed himself to sink very slowly into a chair in front of the TV. Harry's good eye went from Barbara to Ben; his eye fastened on the gun, which Ben lowered butt first to the floor and leaned across his legs. His arm through the fringed sling. Ben maintained his grip on the forepiece. Harry watched.

Helen bent over and placed her hand tenderly on Barbara. "Come on, honey... come and talk to me. It'll make you feel better."

But Barbara made no response. Helen sat down on the other end of the sofa.

Ben remained transfixed before the TV; he was lost in thought, his mind trying to come up with a solution to their dilemma—there was no more kerosene, no vehicle to escape in, and very little ammunition for the rifle. There was nothing on the TV screen; just a dull glow and low hiss of scanning lines and static—he had turned the set on too early.

Harry's good eye was fastened on the gun, the sling wound around Ben's arm.

"Where's your car?" Ben asked, the sound of his voice startling, breaking the virtual silence.

Harry shifted his eye, trying to make it look as though he had not been looking in Ben's direction.

"We were trying to get to a motel before dark," Helen said. "We pulled off the road to look at a map, and those . . . things . . . attacked us. We ran . . . and ran . . ."

"It has to be at least a mile and a half away," Harry said bitterly, as though it satisfied him to see one of Ben's ideas thwarted, even at the cost of his own survival.

"It was all we could do to save Karen," Helen added.

"Do you think we could get to the car?" Ben said. "Is there any chance it would be in the clear, if we could break away from this house?"

"Not a chance," Harry said, flatly.

Ben shouted, angrily, "You give up too easy, man! You want to die in this house?"

"I told you those things turned over our car!" Harry spat.

"It's lying in a gully with its wheels up in the air," Helen said.

"Well . . . if we could get to it, maybe we could do something . . ." Ben conjectured.

"You gonna turn it over by yourself?" Harry said.

"Johnny has the keys . . . keys . . ." Barbara mumbled under her breath.

But nobody heard her—because suddenly there was a loud crackle from the television and the picture and sound faded in.

"GOOD MORNING, LADIES AND GENTLEMEN. THIS IS YOUR CIVIL DEFENSE EMERGENCY NETWORK. EASTERN STANDARD TIME IS NOW THREE A.M.

"IN MOST AREAS AFFLICTED BY THIS . . . TRAGIC PHENOMENON . . . WE ARE SEEING THE FIRST SIGNS THAT IT WILL BE POSSIBLE TO BRING THINGS UNDER CONTROL. CIVILIAN AUTHORITIES WORKING HAND IN HAND WITH THE NATIONAL GUARD HAVE ESTABLISHED ORDER IN MOST OF THE

AFFECTED COMMUNITIES, AND WHILE CURFEWS ARE STILL IN EFFECT, THE INTENSITY OF THE ONSLAUGHT DOES SEEM TO BE RELENTING, AND LAW ENFORCEMENT AGENCIES ARE PREDICTING A RETURN TO NORMALITY WITHIN THE NEAR FUTURE—PERHAPS—WITHIN THE NEXT WEEK.

"DESPITE THIS WORD OF ENCOURAGEMENT, HOWEVER, THE AUTHORITIES WARN THAT A STATE OF VIGILANCE MUST BE MAINTAINED. NO ONE IS CERTAIN HOW LONG THE DEAD WILL CONTINUE TO RISE, OR WHAT WERE THE EXACT REASONS FOR THIS PHENOMENON. ANYONE KILLED OR WOUNDED BY ONE OF THE ... AGGRESSORS ... IS A POTENTIAL ENEMY OF LIVE HUMAN BEINGS. WE MUST CONTINUE TO BURN OR DECAPITATE ALL CORPSES. GRISLY AS THIS ADVICE SOUNDS, IT IS AN ABSOLUTE NECESSITY. DOCTOR LEWIS STANFORD, OF THE COUNTY HEALTH DEPARTMENT, REPEATEDLY EMPHASIZED THIS POINT IN AN INTERVIEW TAPED EARLIER TODAY IN THIS TELEVISION STUDIO ..."

The narrator faded out, as the taped interview faded in Doctor Lewis Stanford, seated behind his desk, was being interviewed by a reporter holding a microphone and wearing a headset.

"DOCTOR, CAN YOU OR YOUR COLLEAGUES SHED ANY LIGHT ON THE CAUSES OF THIS PHENOMENON?"

(The doctor fidgeted in his chair and shook his head.)

"WELL ... NO ... IT'S NOTHING THAT WE CAN READILY EXPLAIN. I'M NOT GOING TO SAY THAT WE WON'T HAVE AN ANSWER FOR YOU IN THE NEAR FUTURE, BUT SO FAR OUR RESEARCH HAS YIELDED NO CONCLUSIVE ANSWERS ..."

"WHAT ABOUT THE VENUS PROBE?"
"THE VENUS PROBE?"
"YES, SIR."
"UH ... I'M ... NOT QUALIFIED TO COMMENT ON THAT."
"BUT THAT IS WHERE MOST OF THE SPECULATION HAS BEEN DIRECTED, SIR."
"STILL AND ALL, I AM NOT AN AEROSPACE EXPERT. I AM UNACQUAINTED WITH THAT PARTICULAR EXPLORATION ATTEMPT. I AM A MEDICAL PATHOLOGIST—"
"WHAT LIGHT CAN YOU SHED ON THIS, DOCTOR?"
"WELL ... I FEEL THAT OUR EFFORTS HAVE BEEN DIRECTED PROPERLY. WE'RE DOING WHAT WE'VE BEEN TRAINED TO DO ... THAT IS, WE ARE TRYING TO DISCOVER A MEDICAL OR PATHOLOGICAL REASON FOR A PHENOMENON THAT IS WITHOUT PRECEDENT IN OUR MEDICAL HISTORY. WE ARE TREATING WHAT HAPPENED TO THESE ... DEAD ... PEOPLE AS A DISEASE WHICH VERY PROBABLY HAS A BIOLOGICAL EXPLANATION FOR IT; IN OTHER WORDS, IT IS MOST LIKELY CAUSED BY MICROBES OR VIRUSES PREVIOUSLY UNKNOWN TO US OR PREVIOUSLY NOT A THREAT TO US, UNTIL SOMETHING HAPPENED TO ACTIVATE THEM. WHETHER OR NOT THE VENUS PROBE HAD ANYTHING TO DO WITH THIS IS SOMETHING WE COULDN'T DETERMINE FOR CERTAIN UNTIL WE ISOLATE THE VIRUS OR MICROBE AND GO TO VENUS AND FIND THAT THEY ACTUALLY EXIST THERE."
"IS THERE A CHANCE THAT WHATEVER IS CAUSING THIS WILL SPREAD—WILL BE WITH US PERMANENTLY NOW? WILL WE HAVE TO GO ON BURNING OUR CORPSES?"
"I DON'T KNOW ... I DON'T KNOW. IT IS POSSIBLE, HOWEVER, THAT THE DISEASED ORGANISMS WHICH

ARE RESPONSIBLE FOR THIS PHENOMENON ARE SHORT-LIVED—THAT IS, THEY MAY ALL DIE OFF IN A SHORT TIME; THEY MAY BE A MUTANT BREED THAT IS NOT CAPABLE OF REPRODUCTION. WE ARE VERY HOPEFUL THAT THIS WILL TURN OUT TO BE THE CASE."

"WHAT CLUES HAVE YOU DISCOVERED SO FAR, DOCTOR STANFORD?"

"OUR RESEARCH IS JUST BEGINNING. EARLIER TODAY, IN THE COLD ROOM AT THE UNIVERSITY, WE HAD A CADAVER—A CADAVER FROM WHICH ALL FOUR LIMBS HAD BEEN AMPUTATED. IN A SHORT TIME AFTER BEING REMOVED FROM THE COLD ROOM, IT OPENED ITS EYES. IT WAS DEAD, BUT IT OPENED ITS EYES AND BEGAN TO MOVE. OUR PROBLEM NOW IS TO OBTAIN MORE SUCH CADAVERS FOR EXAMINATION AND EXPERIMENTATION—WE HAVE TO ASK THE MILITARY PERSONNEL AND THE CIVILIAN PATROLS THAT ARE OUT IN THE FIELD TO STOP BURNING ALL OF THESE THINGS—TO DEACTIVATE SOME AND BRING THEM TO US STILL ALIVE, SO WE CAN STUDY THEM. SO FAR, WE HAVE NOT BEEN SUCCESSFUL IN OBTAINING MANY OF SUCH CADAVERS..."

"THEN HOW DOES THIS FIT IN WITH YOUR TELLING PEOPLE THEY SHOULD BURN OR DECAPITATE ANYBODY, EVEN RELATIVES OR NEXT OF KIN, WHO DIES DURING THIS EMERGENCY?"

"THAT ADVICE STILL HOLDS TRUE FOR THE GENERAL PUBLIC. IF WE ARE TO OBTAIN CADAVERS FOR EXAMINATION, WE WANT TO DO IT IN AN ORGANIZED WAY SO THEY CAN BE HANDLED UNDER STERILE CONDITIONS AND WITH AS LITTLE RISK AS POSSIBLE—BOTH AS TO THE PARTIES INVOLVED AND AS TO THE DANGER OF PROLONGING THIS EMERGENCY. THE PUBLIC IN GENERAL SHOULD CONTINUE TO BURN ALL CORPSES. JUST DRAG

THEM OUTSIDE AND BURN THEM. THEY'RE JUST DEAD FLESH, AND DANGEROUS—"

With this final word from Doctor Stanford, the TV report faded back to the live announcer.

"THAT REPORT, WHICH YOU JUST SAW, WAS TAPED EARLIER TODAY IN OUR STUDIO. RECAPPING DOCTOR STANFORD'S ADVICE IT IS STILL MANDATORY FOR CIVILIANS TO BURN OR DECAPITATE ANYONE WHO DIES DURING THIS EMERGENCY. IT IS A DIFFICULT THING TO DO, BUT THE AUTHORITIES ADVISE THAT YOU MUST DO IT. IF YOU CANNOT BRING YOURSELF TO DO IT, YOU MUST CONTACT YOUR LOCAL POLICE OR PROTECTION AGENCY, AND THEY WILL DO IT FOR YOU.
"NOW OUR TV CAMERAS TAKE YOU TO WASHINGTON, WHERE LATE EVENING REPORTERS SUCCEEDED IN INTERVIEWING GENERAL OSGOOD AND HIS STAFF, AS HE WAS RETURNING FROM A HIGH-LEVEL CONFERENCE AT THE PENTAGON ..."

Again the commentator faded out and newsreel footage faded in—

But, suddenly there was a crash from outside and the lights went out. The screen went blank. The house was submerged in darkness.

Ben's voice rang out:

"Is there a fuse box in the cellar?"

"It's . . . it's not the fuse," Harry stammered. "The power lines must be down!"

Ben squirted charcoal-lighter into the embers of the fire, and with a loud whoosh the flames leapt up. He threw a bundle of rolled-up newspapers onto the fire. Then, in the half-light, he opened the cellar door wide and began to work his way downstairs.

Harry seized Helen by the arm and pulled her face close to his so he could whisper. "Helen... I've got to get that gun. We can go to the cellar. You have to help me!"

He had let the ice pack come away from his eye, and in the flickering light from the fire Helen saw its blackened, swollen condition—and the desperation in his face.

"I'm not going to help you," she whispered hoarsely. "Haven't you had enough? He'd kill us both."

"That man is crazy!" Harry argued, fighting to hold his voice to a whisper. "He's already responsible for two people being dead—I've got to get that gun—"

Harry was cut short by the sound of Ben's footsteps at the top of the stairs, and Ben entered the room. "It's not the fuse box," he announced, with an air of hopelessness. "I had to feel my way to it—but I found a flashlight down there. All the fuses are okay. I left the flashlight at the head of the stairs, so we can see to go down. You'd better go down there and see to your daughter. She'll be—"

Crash! From the kitchen, the sound of splintering glass. Then more racket. Moans and loud crashes. The walls of the house began to shake. The dead things outside were attacking it en masse. Some of them had gotten into the den and were hammering at the barricaded door.

Ben was on his feet immediately, trying to reinforce the barricades. With hammer and crowbar, he swung through the broken glass at the dead things and tried to shore up the pieces of lumber that were threatening to give way under the onslaught.

"Harry! Harry! Give me a hand over here!"

Harry came over behind Ben, and instead of helping ripped the gun from Ben's back. Holding the gun on Ben, Harry backed toward the cellar. Ben turned around, panicked; the things were breaking into the house.

"What are you up to, man? We've got to keep those things out!"

"Now we'll see who's going to shoot who," Harry said, backing away and waving the gun in Ben's direction. "I'm going to the cellar, and I'm taking the two women with me—and you can rot up here, you crazy bastard!"

Ignoring Harry, Ben threw his body against the window, where the barricades were starting to come apart. At least a half-dozen ghouls were outside the window, pounding at it, forcing the nails loose.

Harry froze for a moment, transfixed by the fury of the attack and by Ben's indifference to the fact that he no longer had possession of the rifle; Harry had expected Ben to beg to be allowed to come with the others to the cellar.

Purposely, Ben let the ghouls pry loose one of the largest pieces of lumber that had been nailed across the living room window; then, when it was loose, he spun and hurled it in Harry's direction. The gun was hit and knocked aside, and it fired its shot harmlessly into the floor. Ben leaped upon Harry and, after a brief violent struggle, succeeded in wrenching the gun away.

Helen watched, frozen in place, with the noise of the ghouls pounding in her ears.

Harry backed away from Ben, toward the cellar.

Ben cocked and fired. Harry screamed. A great clot of blood appeared at his chest. Clutching the wound, he began to sink; he fell through the entranceway to the cellar stairs, then reeled and grabbed the banister, staggered, and fell head first down the stairs.

Some ghouls had broken through the window, and they had Helen by the hair and by the neck, ripping and clawing at her. Ben pounded and smashed at them with the butt of the rifle; then he leveled off and shot two of them in the face. Freed, Helen ran screaming to the cellar and, in the absence of light, she too fell and tumbled down the stairs. Her screams grew louder, as she realized she had fallen onto something large and soft—the dead body of her husband; her hand was wet and slippery with his blood. Then, out of the darkness something stumbled toward her, and moaned softly, and clutched at her.

"Karen?"

It was Karen. But she was dead. Her eyes flickered in the dark.

She let go of her dead father's wrist, which she had been holding to her lips; she had been chewing the tender flesh on the underside of his forearm.

Helen struggled to see in the darkness.

"Karen? Baby?"

The dead little girl had a garden trowel. Silently, staring without a word, she plunged the trowel into her mother's chest. Helen fell back, screaming and clutching while the life-blood gushed from her and her daughter began stabbing her again and again. Helen's screams mingled with the other sounds of destruction echoing through the old house.

Then the screams stopped. But the garden trowel continued to stab downward, again and again, hacking Helen's body to bits, rending and tearing the bloody flesh. When the trowel fell from her dead blood-stained hands, Karen bent over her mother, drooling, and bared her teeth . . . She dug her hands into the gaping wounds . . .

Upstairs, Ben was continuing to fight as hard as he could hoping to drive the things back.

With the hysteria of revenge, Barbara too had flung herself into the attack. She smashed a chair against one aggressor, and it went down, and she threw herself upon it and beat her fists into its face—then the thing grabbed her and they rolled and struggled, the dead creature clawing at Barbara and sinking its teeth into her neck. Ben stepped up and pointed his gun directly in the thing's face and fired, and the force of the explosion hurled the thing back, splattering Barbara with blood and bits of bone as the back of her attacker's head was blown off. She jumped to her feet screaming and screaming—and ran straight into a cluster of ghouls that had smashed through the living room door.

The ghouls seized Barbara, ripping and tearing at her and dragging her outside the house. She looked up, as more attackers moved in for the kill, and began to struggle for possession of her soon-to-be-dead body. One of the attackers was her brother, Johnny, back from the dead. He stared evilly, his teeth smashed and his face caked with dried blood and dirt, as he moved toward

Barbara and dug his fingers into her throat. She screamed, and passed out, dead of shock. The ghouls dragged her out into the night, ripping her apart and digging their hands and teeth into the soft parts of her body—while groups of two or three of the flesh-eaters pulled and twisted at her limbs, trying to break and tear bone and cartilage to dismember her body.

Inside the house, Ben was nearly overwhelmed. At least twenty or thirty ghouls were now in the house, the barricades broken through. There was no way that Ben could continue to stand and fight.

For a moment, there was a stand-off as the ghouls stood and stared, confronting the man that they had trapped, like a rat in a corner of a room.

Ben backed toward the cellar door. Then, from behind, the little girl, Karen, seized him, clawing and tearing at him—and he wheeled and grabbed her by the throat and hurled her against the wall—but she got to her feet and advanced toward him, her face smeared with her mother's blood—and the other ghouls, too, had started to advance.

Ben stepped onto the cellar stairs, slamming the door behind him and frantically barricading it as the ghouls pounded and smashed at the door and the walls. The sounds of their rasping breath and their insane pounding and smashing filled Ben's ears as he trembled and hoped that the barricade would hold. Though the pounding continued for a long time, the door seemed to be strong. The ghouls seemed unable to break it down. Ben sat there in the dark—overwhelmed by the hopelessness of his situation and the fact that everybody was dead who had tried to hold out in the old house, everybody but him.

Then his fingers closed around the flashlight that he had left there earlier when he had come to check out the fuse box, and, turning it on and pointing its beam of light ahead of him, he began to descend into the basement.

In the peripheral illumination from the beam of the flashlight, Ben looked at his arm and—with a shock—saw that he was bleeding. The girl, Karen—she had bitten him in their struggle.

Frozen on the stairs, Ben stared at the teeth marks in his arm. If he died, he was going to become—

—unless a cure could be found—

He did not allow his mind to complete the horrible thought of what might happen to him.

The pounding of the ghouls at the cellar door was growing weaker, and more half-hearted.

The flesh-eaters, content to devour and fight over the remains of the slaughtered Barbara, were wandering out of the house, out into the yard—where groups of ghouls were already sinking their teeth into warm human flesh and organs—and gnawing at human bone.

At the foot of the stairs, the beam of Ben's flashlight fell on the ash-white dead face of Harry Cooper, with his arm half chewed through at the elbow.

And slowly in a little while Harry's eyelids began to flutter... and come open...

Chapter 13

The sounds of men braking camp disturbed the normal hush and silence of the woods in the gray dawn. A damp mist hung over the field where the men had slept, and as they straggled to assemble in the clearing which McClellan had designated, white breath hissed from their mouths and nostrils and hovered around them as they walked. They did not talk much, but they stuck close together in little groups, in case one of the dead things should attack them out of the fog.

George Henderson spat on the ground and said to the sheriff, "It's a wonder how it could be so warm last night and so cold this morning. Maybe we got some rain movin' in."

"Naw," McClellan said. "I checked the weather report. The sun'll come up and burn this fog in a few hours."

"It'll be hell if it rains, and these men have to slog through mud," George said. "There'll be some people that won't get rescued."

As the two men talked, a white jeep station wagon, its engine growling, nosed its way in circles through the tall, damp grass—as two posse men, fully armed, followed along behind the jeep—stopping here and there to pick up bed rolls and packed-up tents and throw them on board.

The campfires had all been doused; there were beds of wet,

black coals scattered throughout the field, in proximity to the tents and bed rolls.

"Hurry it up, men!" McClellan yelled. "How'd you like it if your wife or daughter was waitin' for you to haul ass and save her from those things?"

The men stepped it up a little bit.

Soon they were all assembled in the clearing under the trees, where McClellan's tent had been pitched.

Chapter 14

The circle of light on Harry Cooper's face grew larger as Ben descended the staircase. Ben moved the flashlight quickly to take in the whole picture. Harry lay dead in a pool of blood, his arm chewed halfway through. Helen lay dead too, not far away, a garden trowel protruding from her hacked-up chest.

With an additional flutter of his eyelids, Harry opened his eyes wide. Then he began to sit up. Holding the flashlight and the gun at the same time, Ben stepped as close as he dared, and took careful aim. He quivered but pulled the trigger—and was jolted by recoil as the top of Harry's head was blown off and the loud report of the rifle echoed in the dank basement.

Ben looked down, moving the flashlight and pointing it. He shuddered as he thought he could see splatters of blood on the bottoms of his trouser legs.

Then, he remembered Helen—and he pointed the flashlight in her direction. Her face and hair were caked with blood; blood had come in a stream from her mouth and nostrils, and several of her teeth were broken and twisted; her ribs, where some flesh had been eaten away, showed glistening white in the beam of the flashlight. In a little while, she opened her eyes—and Ben fired. Her body heaved and twitched with an abrupt convulsion, as the bullet smacked into her brain.

Ben threw the rifle down and covered his eyes with his hands. Tears rolled down his cheeks as he stepped over the dead bodies. Moving the flashlight around, he was overcome by the loneliness and the dismalness of the dark cellar—and his eyes fell on the makeshift table that had been Karen's sick bed. In a fit of rage, he overturned the table and hurled it to the floor, with a crash. Then he staggered about aimlessly in his grief, stumbling over objects in the dark as though they weren't there if the flashlight failed to show them.

Tom. Judy. Barbara. Harry. Helen.

All dead.

If only the truck hadn't caught fire.

If only...

If only...

Gathering his senses together somewhat, Ben picked up the rifle and cocked it. He looked all around, pointing the gun and the flashlight. His eyes scanned his surroundings for possible areas of threat or vulnerability. Moving around slowly and quietly, holding his breath though it wanted to come gasping out of him, he probed behind the packing crates and in the dark corners of the cellar.

There was nobody around. Nobody in hiding. Just the dead bodies of Harry and Helen Cooper.

Ben sat in a corner, leaning against a wall of concrete block, and cried softly.

He looked down at the wound on his arm. And at the blood splattered on his trousers.

Upstairs, the noise of the ghouls had stopped. Perhaps a few were still in the house, lurking silently.

From exhaustion, finally, Ben's head nodded and he yielded to an agonized, nervous sleep.

His last thoughts were of his children.

Chapter 15

Sunrise.
 Bird sounds. Then the sounds of dogs, and human voices.
 The rising sun, bright and warm. Dew on the high grass of a meadow.
 More sounds, in the distance.
 The whir of a helicopter.
 Men with dogs and guns, working their way up from the woods that surrounded the meadow. Shouts ... muffled talk ... panting and straining of dogs against leashes ... Sheriff McClellan's posse.

Chapter 16

Ben nodded and snapped awake—startled, unsure of his surroundings.

He thought he heard a helicopter. Or maybe he was dreaming. He listened.
Nothing.
Then, in the distance, a beating of metal wings.
A helicopter. Definitely.

Ben clutched the rifle and listened and looked all around. The basement was not dark any longer; but it was not bright, either; it was dusky and dank, illuminated in varying shades of gray by whatever sunlight could filter through the high, tiny windows. The helicopter sounds continued to fade in . . . and recede. Ben strained his ears, but could hear no other signs of human activity.

Finally, stepping gingerly and trying not to look, he got past the corpses of Helen and Harry Cooper and began to sneak up the cellar stairs.

The stairs creaked, startling him, but he paused only momentarily, then continued his ascent toward the barricaded door.

CHAPTER 17

A few men, some German shepherds on leashes, came up out of the woods and onto the edge of the sunlit, dewy meadow. They stopped and looked all around, as if they were scrutinizing the meadow for possible danger. The boots and trouser legs of the men were damp, from plodding through the wet grass.

Sheriff McClellan was the next man up from the surrounding thicket—he was breathing hard because of his weight and the difficult job of leading the men through the woods, when none of them had had any rest or any breakfast. He was armed with his rifle and pistol, with a belt of ammunition slung over his shoulder. He paused, looked back over his shoulder into the woods, and mopped perspiration from his brow with a balled-up dirty handkerchief.

More men were still working their way out of the woods, into the clearing. McClellan shouted at them.

"Come on—let's step it up, now! Never can tell what we'll run into up here—"

His voice broke off as his deputy, George Henderson, came over to him and opened his mouth to say something.

But McClellan spoke first.

"You keeping in touch with the squad cars, George?"

George was wearing a sweatband and carrying a rifle and a

side-arm—and he also had a walkie-talkie strapped on his back. Breathing hard, he hunched and adjusted the straps of his burden. "Yeah . . . they know where we are. They should be intercepting us at the Miller farmhouse."

"Good," McClellan said. "These men is dog tired. They can use some rest and hot coffee . . ." Then, looking back toward the men moving up from behind, he shouted, "Let's push along, now—the squad cars'll be waiting with coffee and sandwiches at the house!"

The men continued to push on, across the meadow. And soon they began to work their way cautiously into the strip of woods on the other side.

CHAPTER 18

At the top of the cellar stairs, Ben was listening as intently as he could, behind the barricade.

For a long time, he had not been able to hear any helicopter sounds; perhaps it had landed somewhere, or flown away. Ben wished he could have been upstairs, so he could wave to it from the lawn.

Then—from far off—he heard the distinct sound of a dog—barking. He listened for a long time, but heard nothing more. He was tempted to undo the barricade and take his chances on going out there to look around.

Chapter 19

When the men worked their way through the narrow belt of trees on the far side of the meadow, they came out into a cemetery, the one Barbara and John had come to with the wreath for their father. The posse continued its advance, threading its way among the grave markers.

Down a dirt road, and up a short grade, the men found Barbara's car, with the smashed window. The headlight switch was on, but the battery was dead. There were no signs of blood, and the men could not find any corpses anywhere near the car.

"Maybe whoever was in here escaped and got away," McClellan said, hopefully. "Move on, men! We can't do any good here!"

The men passed through the cemetery and out onto the two-lane blacktop road, where several squad cars were parked, waiting. There were also one or two motorcycle patrolmen, and one of them dismounted and hailed McClellan.

"Hi, Sheriff! How's things goin'?"

McClellan advanced, mopping his brow, and stopped to shake hands with the motorcycle patrolman. Meanwhile, the men in the posse began to catch up and regroup.

McClellan said, "Sure glad to see you fellas, Charlie. We been at it damn near all night—but I don't want to break till we get to the Miller house over there. We might be screwin' around while somebody needs our help—we'll see, first, then stop and get some coffee."

"Sure, Sheriff."

The two men looked around at the gathering posse, which was beginning to fill up the neck in the blacktop road.

"Get started over that wall and through that field!" George Henderson shouted, with the walkie-talkie on his back. "The Miller farmhouse is over there!"

He took the time to unsling the walkie-talkie and hand it to one of the cops in a squad car. Then, leading a squad of men, he began to move toward the field in front of the Miller house.

Gunshots rang out almost immediately.

"Ghouls! Ghouls—all over the place!" a voice yelled. A bevy of gunshots split the air. More men moved up, running and firing from behind trees.

The police dogs growled and strained at their leashes, hating the scent of the dead things.

The posse advanced in squads, across the field and toward the shed with the gasoline pumps—where several of the flesh-eaters were lurking and trying to get away, but they were gunned down.

Nearer the house, there were still more ghouls, and firing repeatedly, the squads of men moved forward, felling the dead things with a trail of bullets.

There were more of the creatures, trying to hide in and around a burned-out truck—but they were unsuccessful; they tried to run, but the posse gunned them down.

Each time a ghoul fell, one of the men moved forward and hacked at it with a machete, until the head was severed from the body. That way, they knew the ghoul would not get to its feet again.

For better than half an hour, the echo of gunshots was constant in the fields surrounding the old Miller farmhouse.

Chapter 20

Still at the top of the cellar stairs, Ben knew for sure now that there were men outside. The gunshots were undeniable. And he even thought he had heard a car engine. But he was afraid to open the door, because some of the creatures might still be in the house. Yet... he knew he was going to have to open the door...

Slowly, quietly, he began undoing the heavy barricades...

Chapter 21

McClellan fired, and the dead thing fifty feet in front of him clutched at its face with a convulsive movement and toppled to the earth, like a sack of potatoes, with a dull thud.

More gunshots rang out. And two more of the ghouls fell heavily to the ground.

"Get up here, boys!" McClellan yelled. "There's three more for the fire!"

The men with machetes moved up and hacking quickly and furiously, severed the heads from the dead ghouls.

The sheriff and his men had advanced to the lawn of the old farmhouse and were crouching and firing repeatedly, blasting down the dead creatures that surrounded the place.

"Shoot for the eyes, boys!" McClellan cried out. "Like I told you before . . . always aim right for the eyes!"

The flurry of gunfire was constant—crack—crack! crack!—as the posse surrounded the house.

Then there was silence, as all the ghouls had apparently been felled, and the men's eyes scanned the old place and its environs, looking for a new target to gun down.

Suddenly, from the house—a loud noise. George Henderson had moved up beside McClellan, and the two of them watched and listened, frozen in their tracks.

"There's something in there," Henderson said, unnecessarily. "I heard a noise."

Inside, ready to shoot or swing, Ben had slammed open the cellar door. The force of his shoulder against the door had carried him into the living room, which was empty—there were no ghouls lurking there; there was only the ramshackle destruction from the recent siege. Ben edged his way through the twisted wreckage and overturned furniture toward the front door. There was no light in the place; despite the early morning sunlight, it remained dark under the heavy foliage of the surrounding trees. Some of the barricades partially remained, although weakened and widened for entry by the marauding ghouls. Ben's hands crept to what was left of a curtain; he pulled it back and started to peek out... but... a shot rang out—and Ben reeled, driven back—a circle of blood on his forehead, right between his eyes.

Simultaneously, McClellan shouted:

"Damn it, what'd you shoot for? I told you to be careful—there might be people in there!"

The posse member who had fired the shot said, "Naw, you can see this place is demolished. Anybody in there'd be dead. And if they're dead—"

Several men, led by George Henderson, advanced to kick in the front door. They stepped back and peered cautiously inside. Their faces searched the room. A patch of sunlight from the opened door fell partially on Ben. He was dead. The men looked down at him without pity, as they stepped past him to the cellar. They did not know he was a man.

Squads of men began to enter the house, moving cautiously through the rooms in military fashion, checking for possible aggressors lurking inside.

Two men with machetes came forward and began hacking at Ben, severing his head from his body.

"Somebody put up a good fight here," McClellan said to George Henderson later, when they were sipping black coffee on the front lawn, near a squad car. "It's a damn shame they couldn't hold out a while longer."

"I wonder who it was," Henderson replied, taking a bite of his sandwich. "It wasn't Mrs. Miller. We found what was left of her—upstairs in her room. But we didn't find any trace of her grandson."

"I guess we ain't never going to know," said the sheriff, "but then again there's lots of things we ain't going to know about this damned business."

CHAPTER 22

Ben's head and body were heaved onto the bonfire with the rest. And the meat-hook was yanked out of his chest, with a hard tug on the part of the gloved hand that was yanking it.

Then the lumber and the dead bodies were drenched in gasoline by still another pair of gloved hands.

And the touch of a flaming torch set the whole thing ablaze.

The men stared into the broiling hot fire, and watched flesh curling and melting from dead bone, much as the paint curls and melts from a burning blackening page of newsprint. They backed away from the heat finally and went to where they could discard their meat-hooks and gloves and wash their hands in sterile alcohol.

But they could not escape the stench of burning flesh.

Printed in Poland
by Amazon Fulfillment
Poland Sp. z o.o., Wrocław